THE ORIGIN OF DELUSIONS

N.M. BROWN

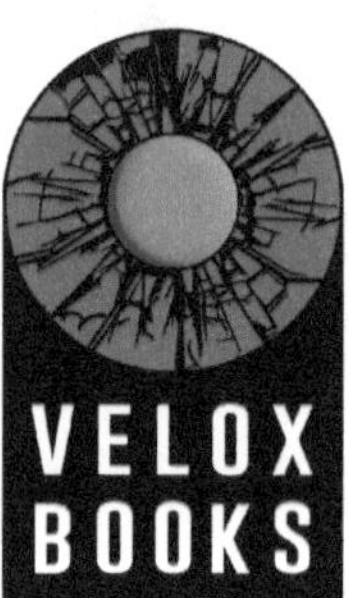

Published by arrangement with the author.

Copyright © 2025 by N.M. Brown.

All rights reserved.

**FOLLOW VELOX TO KEEP
THE NIGHTMARES COMING:**

CONTENTS

ACKNOWLEDGEMENTS AND DEDICATIONS

There are so many people to thank for helping me get where I am today.

First, I would like to thank my husband Kevan, who has supported me through the good times and bad. Thank you for being tough when I need it and always letting me (and anyone who will listen) know how proud you are of me.

Next, I would like to dearly thank my children—Aidan, Logan and Evan Dean. I hope one day (not too soon) you will read this and know just how much your mother loved you. I aspire to greatness to show you the way. Hopefully you won't look at your ole' Ma too weird after reading these.

Next—the cornerstone of my heart: my family. We didn't have the easiest lives, but we never lost our sense of humor OR… sense of what was most important: Family.

To my father George—who ALWAYS believed I could be more… do more. I've become one of the best because of the lessons you've taught me about working hard and fulfilling my potential. To my sisters Diana and Melanie—whether it be introducing me to the Nightmare on Elm Street series and Halloween IV or having junk food sleepovers while binging Tales from the Crypt, you both are my heart and soul. You've supported and prepared me more for my journey than you will ever possibly know.

To my Aunt Christine, who shared my love of the weird or horrific. Thank you for always helping me find the humor in the darkness. I hope you're proud of what I've been doing.

To my mother and grandmother—the original Gaga,

I love and miss you both more than you will know.

To my employer, inspiration and mentor Jon Grilz—You shared your dream with me and accepted me into your Creepy world with open tentacles. You inspire me to be the best writer, coordinator and podcast employee I can be. Thanks for taking a chance on this gal!

To all of the writing groups that have read my work, shared theirs and have welcomed me into their hearts—Thank you! I have met some of the very best friends I have made in my life through here.

To all of my friends and readers—there are far too many to name individually, but I truly would be nothing without you.

THE ROADSIDE MEMORIAL

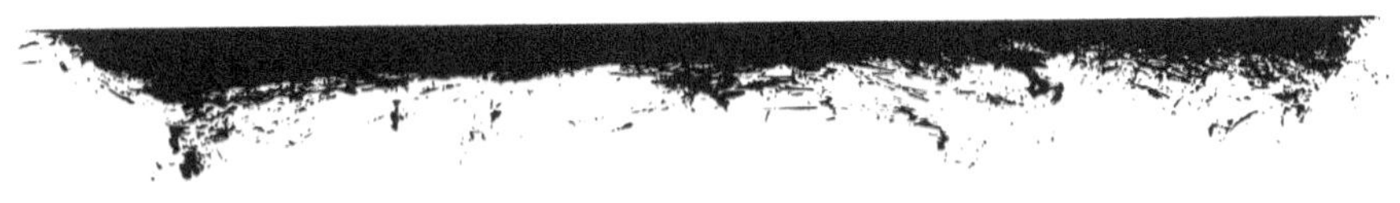

You know those people who you tell the time of events to fifteen minutes early because you know they'll be late? The people who would be late to their own funerals, as the saying goes. Well... that's me. Prepare as I might, I can never seem to get anywhere on time. It's the most frustrating trait ever, yet it's absolutely always my fault. It hasn't always been this way.

Before I had my daughter Brynn almost nine months ago, I was one of those people who took punctuality very seriously; the kinda guy who looked at the traffic flow on his phone and made sure to get gas the day before. I even set my oven clock 5 minutes fast so there would always be a five-minute advantage. I was prepared for most obstacles.

However, what I couldn't prepare for was the unpredictability of Brynn. Her needs and moods varied like all babies do. There was no rhyme or reason to her play. She did what she wanted when she wanted, no matter if it made sense or not. It's like she was saying, "No, Dad. I will lay here and eat my foot for exactly one minute and twenty-seven seconds. If you attempt to remove it before this time passes, you will be met with total noncooperation." Not to mention the crying and flailing of the limbs.

We had a good enough routine before her mother left us about three months ago. I'm ashamed to admit I threw away the outfit our daughter was wearing the day that she left. Over the preceding weeks, she had been donating a lot of her things to Goodwill. Supposedly it was to make more room in our closet; my wife said she was trying to be less materialistic for the new year. It turns out she'd been moving her things to another house.

Newfound parenthood hadn't been going well for us. I told her to take a night out with her friends while I spent one-on-one time with Brynn. When I kissed her goodbye that night, I had no idea she'd never be coming back. Since then, the baby and I have just tried to make the best of our situation and establish new routines.

⸻

These are the thoughts running through my head as I rush to Brynn's nine-month doctor checkup. We are early for once, set and out the door. Then, naturally, she pokes the nipple through her bottle and pours it all over herself.

So, we go back into the house, clean her up and repeat the process. It's 9:19 and her appointment is at 9:30. It will easily take twenty minutes to get there and that's with cooperative traffic. I'm not going to super speed or lane weave just to be on time. We will just have to be a little late… again… as usual.

We're almost there; there are only about five miles left. I start to allow myself to relax my shoulders a little when Brynn starts wailing. Oh, Christ, not again. *Not now*, I think to myself, figuring she poked through her bottle again. You can't take a dirty baby to the doctor ever, but especially not for a checkup. It just doesn't look right; it isn't right.

The pitch and repetition of her screaming is making my head feel like a kettle that's about to boil. Before it reached its crescendo of shrill whistling, I pulled over. If I knew then what I know now, I would never have stopped or would have pulled into the nearest gas station. Anything other than where I choose to stop at.

I prepare to pull off the road and get out of the car to open the door of the back seat. There she is, snotty and red-faced. Her blonde curls are sticking to her face with the sweat of frustration. My little sweetheart, she looks just like her mother when she cries. It makes me sad; but I can't think about that now. She knew what she was doing when she left us. No sense in keeping her ghost around, especially in my own head.

It turns out we pulled over next to a little roadside memorial. A slightly worn but still silver and pink cross is placed there with flowers withered by the hands of time and various other trinkets of memorial. The name on the cross reads Emily Semple. It looks like a child's; that makes me sadder to think about then when I think about my wife. *It's something at least,* I thought. A temporary mental vacation into someone else's hell to be able to escape my own.

I look her over and thankfully she hasn't spilled her bottle. Maybe we still have a chance of being somewhat on time. I hand her the bottle back, wipe her face, and kiss her forehead. Thinking if I show her love it will help calm her down. As if she could read my mind, she threw her bottle, and it bounced off my forehead and onto the floor. Great.

I haven't realized how much of a shameful mess my car has become. Napkins, empty bottles, condiment wrappers, baby toys and maybe even a French fry or two litter the seats and floorboards. In my effort to retrieve the bottle, I knocked some things out of my car onto the roadside. The wind starts to blow some of them into the road. So, not wanting to travel too far away from the car, I grab what I can and stuff the items back into the backseat on the floor, to be cleaned or forgotten about later.

We make it to the doctor's office a whopping 20 minutes late. I sheepishly grin and apologize, hoping they can still see her, and I don't have to make another appointment to come back. The front desk ladies' voices were understanding, but their eyes certainly had not been. Perhaps they softened when they saw me juggling a baby car seat with a very loud pink diaper bag falling off my shoulder repeatedly as I tried to continue to calm her down. Yes, she was still wailing away.

A nurse with a worn face but kind eyes came over to us. "Now, now, little lady, what seems to be the matter? That face is too beautiful to be scrunched up screaming like that. Are you hungry? Do you want Daddy to rock you?" She turns her gaze to me with a smile. "Why don't you take her out, Daddy, and bounce her in your arms a bit? Some babies just hate to be in their car seats any longer than they have to be."

I smile, thank her, and take her advice. Just as I get her out and sit down with her, the door opens. "Michael Hollander and baby Brynn, we are ready to see you now. Come on back to room 4 with the white and yellow clouds."

I gather up all our things and head back to the room, Brynn finally settles down and snuggles into my shoulder. Her thumb's in her mouth so I knew all was well in Brynn-ville. That's one of her happy places. 'Taking the thumb train to Brynn-ville' her mom used to say.

Two vaccinations and a few spoons of ice cream later we pull back in the driveway, ready to recover from the whole ordeal. As I pull her seat out of the car, I notice a little pink elephant with a yellow star on its side. I pick it up and hand it to her as I take her in the house. She coos appreciatively as she grabs onto it.

Hmmm... I don't remember buying this for her. It probably came from her grandmother's house. She always dotes on her. Every time she is out and sees something baby-ish she always gets it for her. "It was just too cute, and Mimi couldn't leave it there when Brynn would love it so much," she says.

Reena, or 'Mimi" as she proclaims herself, is Brynn's maternal grandmother. Since my wife left us, she's gone above and beyond to step up and be there. I think it makes her feel better about the whole situation. As if she somehow feels responsible for her daughter's selfishness and actions.

My mother is long gone, and Reena is such a beautiful part of Brynn's life. I would never do anything to take that away from either of them. It's hard to find people you trust to help you. And it's become so hard to do on my own. I'm so thankful for every second with my baby, but I definitely wasn't expecting to raise her on my own. That was never the plan.

Speaking of, my phone rings and it's Reena calling. She had told me to call her after the appointment was over and I had forgotten. I quickly try to think of a somewhat acceptable excuse while I place Brynn in her crib. Coming up with nothing and mentally exhausted, I answered the phone.

"Hello?" I answer.

"Hey Michael, how did Baby—girl's appointment go today? You know how I worry about our princess," she asked me.

"A couple shots and some tears. Nothing a little ice cream couldn't fix. She's in the 78th percentile for height and 74th for weight and doc says she is doing beautifully." I replied proudly.

I can hear a subtle sigh of relief from her end of the phone. "Good. I am glad she is doing ok. Do you both have plans for the day?" There's a hopeful tone in her voice as she asks this. "No, not really, I am just going to get some cleaning done and maybe head out to the store later to fill up the freezer."

She makes a subtle sound of disapproval. "Mike, you can't take her out running around all over. She just got shots today and you don't know how she will handle them. Why don't you bring her over here for the day? That way you can do your shopping and clean the house in peace while we have Mimi and Brynn time."

After the meltdown and outfit changes earlier, Mimi time does sound like a good idea. I would miss her, but I could get so much more done and maybe even take a nap. She will most likely sleep most of the day anyway as she always does on shot days. I agree and tell her we will be over in about half an hour. That gives me time to feed her lunch, pack her back up and bring her over.

I start up the car, turn the radio up a little, and head down the road. It's a beautiful day and for once, I don't mind driving. It will all be worth it once I come home from Reena's. Besides, I get to spend the drive fantasizing about the forbidden daytime nap I get to take later.

I stop at what seems to be the hundredth stop light (even though it was really only the 3rd). Tom Petty's velvet voice comes across the radio, so I reach down to turn up the volume even more. The light turns green and I start to accelerate, humming along and excited to get to her grandmother's house.

Suddenly, I feel a shock powerful enough to move my whole car. A deafening screech of metal-on-metal grinds in my ears. It feels as though my teeth are broken and cutting my cheeks from the inside. The car flips once, twice, I feel my head bounce off the steering wheel. All I can think about is my back seat. The car comes to a stop on its hood. My body is burning with white hot pain. Warm, thin blood runs into my eyes as I try to survey my surroundings and stay awake.

What I initially thought were loose teeth, was broken glass from my window. It cut the thin tissue of my chapped lips as I spit it through them. I must have gotten hit, possibly T-boned, I started to fear. My head swims and my eyes become heavy. The dust inside my car starts to float around me in slow motion, and I feel like a computer shutting down one application at a time. I am trying to use all my senses to help me.

I hear nothing. There is no crying, no screaming. For the first time ever, I am terrified at the sound of her silence. I manage to look back at the one mirror fastened to the backseat that survived the crash. I see my little angel in the back seat, upside down, firmly secured in her car seat, motionless. I could fool myself into thinking she's sleeping if not for her neck bent at an unnatural angle and the blood that coats her entire car seat.

The last thing I see before I lose consciousness is a little, red haired girl standing on the smoking road in front of my windshield.

Her face is dirty and caked with dried blood. She is wearing what I guess must have been at one time a white dress with yellowed daisies on it. Her broken finger points accusingly at me through my broken windshield. The hatred of her gaze is the last thing I feel as I begin to fade away...

My eyes shoot open with a startled breath as the phone rings. I strangely find myself at home in my chair. A mixture of relief, disbelief, and surrealism washes over me as I take in my current reality. I jolt to a standing position and run to my mirror, examining my head where it hit the steering wheel. There's nothing, no pain, no bruises or cuts, nothing. Confused but hopeful, I run to Brynn's room; thankful to see that she's sleeping peacefully in her crib.

Either I am losing my mind or that was the most realistic dream I have EVER had. I rush to her, not even caring if I wake her. She wakes up and is smiling at me. Her little hand drops something as I lift her up. I look down to see the little pink elephant with the yellow star. I must have fallen asleep after her appointment today.

The phone rings again and startles me. My heart springs to life thinking it might be my wife. Maybe her mom is calling to check on her, to say that she misses us. That she lost her mind and wants to come back.

I look at my phone and it's Reena. I don't answer and let it go to voicemail. I am still shaken up from that... experience and need to get my shit together. There is no way she won't hear it in my voice and ask questions; I will call her later.

My phone then buzzes with a text message. It's Reena, not wanting to take silence for an answer, and it says: *Hey Michael, just calling to check on Brynn's doctor's appointment today. If you don't have anything going on, please bring her over. I would love to spend the day with her. Talk to you soon.*

Well, I'm definitely NOT going to be driving anywhere after what happened earlier. It will be a miracle if I don't see that image every time I close my eyes for the next five years. I'm not about to turn a foreboding dream into a reality. So, I decided that Brynn and

I will have a much-needed lazy day. I turned on some Netflix for me and my kiddo. I pop some popcorn for myself and sit down next to her on the couch.

I let her snuggle into me and we settled in like that for a little while. Halfway through devouring my popcorn bowl, she starts to eye it. She would look from me to the bowl and then back again. I withdraw it from her reach and tell her no softly. She lets out an irritated grunt and furrows her brow, once again looking towards my bowl. Smiling at her spunk and at this point, just thankful to have her breathing and alive, I let her have a piece.

I walk to the bathroom, satisfied that she's at peace in one spot for once. I'm only in there for one minute... two at most. The living room is silent, and my sweet Brynn is on the floor, looking under the couch with her butt in the air.

I wait back a moment to see what she is doing, figuring she will pull some lost 'treasure' out of there and try to eat it. But much to my horror, she doesn't move. My heart drops as the air around me dissipates. I walk over to her as I call out to her. "You spilled Dada's popcorn monkey butt. Did you find something good under there?" She doesn't respond, doesn't move, doesn't breathe.

My heart drops as I rush to her. I pick her up and roll her over as fast as I can without hurting her. She flops over onto her back like a limp doll and her face is blue. I looked over to the tipped over popcorn bowl, devastated at how stupid I was. I try everything I've ever read about babies and choking. I turned her upside down and hit her on the back. I try to put my fingers down her throat to remove the obstruction. There is nothing... nothing that I can do. It's just me, her lifeless body, and the pink elephant at her feet. Tears sting my eyes as regret stabs my heart with a barbed blade.

I moan and scream in agony as I fumble my cell phone to call 911. My head spins as I start to lose my breath. I look out of my window and again I see the little girl wearing the dress with daisies outside on the street, staring in the direction of my house. Things tilt sideways as the ground rushes up to meet me. I fade away....

I wake up, again to my phone ringing and once again I let it go to voicemail. My heart is beating so fast that I can hardly catch my breath. I am very much still in the situation my mind was just put in. No surprise, it's Reena again. Or… maybe for the first time?

I'm not even sure at this point, honestly. I can't think straight. I have seen things no parent should ever have to see. The baby that I've fought through so much heartache to stay strong for is taken from me again and again. Who is that little girl in the dress? Why is this happening to us? Once again, I rushed to Brynn's room. I'm all too pleased to see that once again she is there sleeping, holding the pink elephant in her hand. I take it away and set it off to the side. She wakes up, her sleepy eyes sparkling, and smiles at me. I bend down, reaching out to touch her as she reaches her hand up to me, slowly falling back to sleep.

I let the Hell we've been stuck in this week to melt away, soaking up her smile. Whatever is going on, whatever hell I was stuck in right now, we were here. Right now, we are very much alive and safe. Today we won't do anything. There will be no car trips, no popcorn, no toys in her crib, no anything that can hurt my little girl. It's my only job in life to protect her and I'll die trying.

The same text message appears from Reena as before, and I decide to call her back. I try to sound as calm as I can, mentioning the same details about the doctor's appointment. This time, however, I decline the offer to come over, deciding not to tell her about the horrifying events of the day. If I doubt my own sanity at this point, why shouldn't she?

After catching up for a bit, we arrange for me to drop Brynn off the next Sunday and she asks, "What is Mimi's baby-girl doing right now?"

I reply "She is asleep in her bed holding onto that elephant. Hey, you have no idea how much she loves that. Where did you find it?"

There is a pause. "Michael, I never got her any elephant toy. I would have remembered." I make an excuse about Brynn waking up and hang up the phone, feeling dazed.

I go to my sweet Brynn. I've decided that I will take her to my room and put her in bed with me all day, where nothing can hurt us. We just must make it through the day and this nightmare will be over. I approach my baby's crib, and she is still there. Only now she lays silent, not moving, not breathing. The silken skin on her arms is cold to the touch. *Not again... not again!* Although at this point, I've seen this far too many times than I am comfortable with, the fear is always embedded in the back of my mind that this may be the last time. Maybe this time I'll pass out, wake up and my little girl will still be gone.

I frantically look around the room for something to hit myself with. Something, anything to make me pass out so we can begin this again. So, I can have my Brynn again. I lost her mother, which still haunts me to this day. I cannot and will not lose her too. Where she goes, I go. She is my only light left in this world.

It turns out I don't have to find anything. I feel my breath slow and the room tilt. The angry eyes of the little girl in the dress follow me all the way to the floor. The more I see her, the more translucent and decomposed her form appears. My worst fear is that by the time there's nothing left, Brynn's chances will run out. I can't let that happen.

The phone rings. I wake up and ignore the call; you know the drill. I run to my daughter and wake her up as gently as I can. Only one thing matters today, the only thing that can fix this. We unintentionally disturbed Emily's resting place. The only chance that we have is to return this to where it came from. I stumble my way to the car with her and hastily strap her into her car seat.

We take off in the direction of her doctor's office. I just pray I get there in time, with no red lights and no accidents. I see the pink and silver cross and immediately pull over. The contents of my stomach empty themselves down the side of my car as I rush out of it. I open the back door and grab the elephant from Brynn's little hands.

Her eyes go big, and her lip puffs out with the threat of on-coming tears. That doesn't matter now, though; I have what I need. As it leaves her hands, it starts raining. I look to the sky, torrents of droplets stabbing at my eyes, and scream. "I'm sorry Emily! We didn't mean to steal from you! Please, leave my baby alone! I never meant to take it! She deserves to live!" There are tears falling from my eyes as spit flies from my lips. "PLEASE!"

With my free hand raised in surrender, I gently place the elephant next to the cross and back away. It may just be in my head, but I swear the air feels lighter, giving me the refreshment of promise. I hope to God that I did the right thing. Brynn and I just need to make it through one whole day.

YOU HAVE NEW MESSAGES

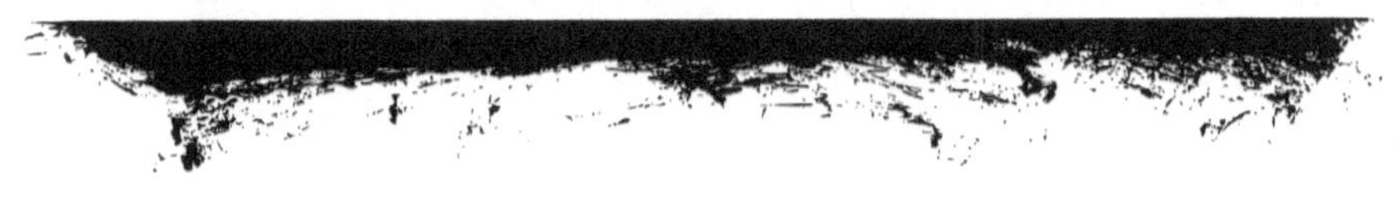

"Hey, you've reached Aaron and Katie. We aren't home right now, but leave us a message and we will get back to you! Thanks!"

"Katie, this is your mother. You didn't call last night and missed lunch with us today. I am getting very worried. Please call us back, OK?"

I listen to the message and look at my wife's face, eyes glazed over, and lips contorted. Her fingers fall limply from their grasp on my arm. My hands continue to shake even after I let go of her neck and she drops to the floor. Rage still burns through my veins while my heart continues to break.

You're probably wondering what happened or why I find myself in the situation that I'm in. You also may already think that I'm a terrible person. Before you jump to any definite conclusions, let me tell you the whole story of how I got here.

Katie and I met in our early 20s and she says it was love at first sight. She said she noticed me before I noticed her. We hung out after work one night and that night turned into a relationship that lasted eight years. She entered my bed and never left it. We seldom left each other's side. We lived together right away, always hung out together, and we even worked together at a few jobs over the years.

We had a wonderful five years or so until we started to try to have children. That's when her depression started. She would withdraw and go quiet. Her silence was like ice: too cold for me to touch. I couldn't understand why things couldn't still be happy with just us. I know how badly she wanted to be a mother, but we still had each other. We had a connection we dreamt about for most of our young lives that some people never find. We started out with just the two of us and were happy. We could still be happy, just the two of us.

After about two years, I made an appointment with a fertility clinic. We both needed to be checked to see what the holdup was. They were able to find that her Fallopian tubes were ravaged with cysts. They had to be removed. Right along with any hope or chance we had of having our own biological child.

Honestly, as terrible as it sounds to say, I am glad we went. Not because of the result, but because they were able to find a problem that Katie had and fix it.

I tried to be there for her, tried to sympathize and help her cope. The upcoming winter season didn't seem to be helping either. We tried marriage counseling and individual therapy for her.

I even spoke to a few adoption lawyers to ask about the process to give us options. It's not what we... *she* had planned, but I always support her and her dreams. If she wanted a baby and I couldn't give it to her, then this seemed the next best option to me.

She wouldn't hear of it, of course. Adoption was like a dirty word to her. She actually cringed when I first said it to her. She couldn't handle the idea of raising someone that she didn't nurture and grow in her womb. Forget about saving another child's quality of life. She was too narcissistic for that.

"I'll only be a disappointment to them, Aaron. If I don't feel that connection, they will sense it and that's not fair to them. You raise a child for the majority of its life and that's just fine. However, when they get to a certain age, they want to know all about their birth parents. They want to know everything about them. You have no idea how many birth parents pop up 'wanting to know their kids' and wouldn't you know, it always seems to happen after they turn 18," she would say.

No matter how I went about the situation, it always ended in tears, nights on the couch and the silence of a frostbitten atmosphere.

She seemed to have started to come around after about a couple of months. I came home and found her listening to music and swirling around the kitchen tiles in her socks. She had painted her fingernails a metallic baby blue. "In honor of wintertime!" She told me excitedly.

To me, her painting her nails was a great thing. If she was pampering herself, she was happy, she was present. She was my Katie again. I couldn't help but smile when I saw the woman that I had married so many years ago.

She even told me she joined a social media group about infertility and loved the support she was getting. It gave her strength to hear other people's struggles and get to share our own with people who utterly understood. I was happy for her.

I wanted to tell her that I was there for her too, and I also understood. That if she shared with anyone it needed to be me, her partner. I was the other person sitting in the chair when the doctor told us. I had visions and dreams crushed too! She didn't need to hear that right now though. Now she was happy, so I was happy.

She certainly was getting support. Her phone would constantly vibrate with notifications and messages, sometimes at all hours of the night. I figured well, it was a big group, and it's not the same time everywhere in the World. She must have set it to notify her every time someone posts something or likes something of hers. She needs support from women right now who understand.

Katie took it very seriously. I'd hand over her phone when it was near me and went off. She would give me looks. Looks like a kid gives his peeking neighbor during a test before he covers his paper so he can't copy.

"Hey, babe," she said looking at me with dancing eyes, "Ya know, some of the women of the group are talking about picking a weekend and doing a spa meet and greet. To put more people in contact with each other and for women to get pampered and cry on each other and things like that. It's not like we have to find anyone to watch our kids," she tried to joke with a pained smile. "Does this sound like something you would like to go to with me?"

I knew if I hesitated too long it was going to be bad one way or another. I would have had to take off work.

God knows where this meeting place was going to be. The chances that it would have been in our city, hell, our state even, were slim to none. Honestly, all of the crying would be so unsettling and awkward for me.

Yes, I did love my wife. She's the only one I have ever loved in my life. However, infertility was already something I had made peace with and accepted months ago. I couldn't bring the level of understanding to the table that was needed for this.

"Uhh... would you like me to, honey, or do you need to be with your new women friends? I honestly want to go and support you if you need me. Though it would be super awkward if I was one of the only men there. There are men in this group, right?"

When I said this, she tried to stifle a giggle by biting her lower lip. She shook her head *no* and then burst into giggles, apologizing in between breaths. "Not really, no. There are just a couple and those are mainly joint accounts. Aaron, you don't have to go. I will totally be ok and understand, but I think this will really help me. Besides, this will give us a chance to miss each other. I'm sure I will come back as a refreshed woman. I don't think you're UN-supportive or uncaring."

It turned out that it was two weeks away in the next state over. From where we were located, it would only take her three and a half hours by car. She would have no problem getting there and having her weekend and then driving back when she woke up on Monday.

I was going to surprise her by making a meal plan and rearranging the living room while she was gone. I wanted to take care of all of the little tasks she nagged me about, but I never got to while I had the time to myself.

The time came for her to leave, and I sent her off with a kiss and my favorite T-shirt. I told her, "You wear this on your saddest cry day. I want to still be the one to wipe your tears even if I can't be there." Again, she got a pained look on her face, but she shook it off with a smile. "Thank you for understanding. I will miss you and will call you every day," she told me. I kissed her and then she left, driving off into her weekend of healing.

After picking up and cleaning the floors, I was almost ready to start rearranging our living room. I had been putting off cleaning the dust from the ceiling and fans for way too long. Neither of us really wanted to do it but I was the taller one, so the task generally fell to me. She would be so happy. She'd be proud that I did that when she came home; a refreshed Katie coming home to a refreshed house.

She called at around nine pm and let me know that she got there alright and that she missed me already. She blew phone kisses after a knock at the door. "Hey, that's my friend. I'll call you in the morning, OK? I love you," she said before getting off the phone. I hoped this would help her and help us be what we once were.

Around the middle of the next day (Saturday) she informed me that her phone was dying. I looked at the counter and saw both of our wall chargers laying there. So, I called her and told her to just use the car charger but not to leave it in while the car was turned off because *A)* someone could steal her phone, and *B)* it could kill her battery.

I missed her and would do so, but I really didn't want to have to drive three hours just to jump her car just to drive home again. She didn't know cars and you can't always depend on strangers, especially another state away. Even if it was only hours from home.

She promised me that she would be fine. That she couldn't talk long, but she loved me and missed me like crazy. For the rest of the day when I called, it would go to voicemail. I was just thankful she was able to tell me what had happened so I wasn't worried, when I suddenly couldn't reach her. It was thoughtful of her to let me know so I wouldn't lose my mind with worry. I mean, she hadn't ever met these people before; they could have been anyone. Who knows the conclusions my mind would have jumped to? I should have made sure that she packed the charger, I thought at the time.

I sent her a *'Have fun! Our bed is cold without you.'* text from work. I wanted my message of love to be the first thing she saw when her phone had more battery life. I couldn't wait to smell her hair again. Before long, it was Monday, the day she was to come home! We chattered excitedly on the phone while she packed.

Before long, I rushed off the phone to get last-minute things ready for her arrival. Our home missed her as much as I did, I think. It was so much darker without her here; the emptiness swallowing me. I would be glad to have her here in my arms. I bought some 'reunited and it feels so good' alcohol for us to enjoy and then went home and waited.

She walked through the door and I gave her a hug that lifted her off of the ground. She did look different. I couldn't place it, but it was different. It almost had the glow of her being centered, finally able to find some peace with herself. I was glad about that. We had both needed that for her. Seeing her so rejuvenated made me feel the same, and we relished our time together. We were so wrapped up that she completely forgot to say anything about the house. That's OK though; she's here now, and that's all I ever wanted.

The holidays came and went, with Katie seeming like a bulb growing brighter every day. I was thankful she was able to turn it into positivity. For some childless couples, the holiday season can be a big slap in the face. Her group even did a Secret Santa, one of the members sending Katie a very name brand, awfully expensive, very... out of our budget gift. I was happy for her; she deserved nice things. She really lucked out on her Secret Santa.

One day I got a call when Katie was in the shower. It was her mom saying that her father was having some chest pain, so she was taking him to the hospital. I relayed the message to her, and she rushed out. I handed her some clothes, her purse, and the keys. I lovingly told her to keep me updated on her way out. I hoped that my father-in-law was going to be ok. I would have gone with her, but I had work in a little over an hour.

I heard a buzzing and looked around our room to see where it was coming from. It sounded like a phone, but I checked my phone and it wasn't me. I get on the floor and peer under the bed and there is Katie's phone. It probably fell out of her purse when I picked it up to hand it to her. I couldn't help myself; I unlocked her screen. What I saw made the color drain from my body and curdled my stomach instantly.

Katie: *I had so much fun this weekend. I can't believe how amazing everything was. I didn't even want to sleep! It's crazy how well things went. Now we know.*

Allen: *Oh my god me too. I felt so comfortable with you. Three and a half days. It's like we have been together for years.*

Katie: *I think this 'group' is going to have monthly meetings if I can manage. We have been talking for so long. Then we met and it was like an instant connection. I can't wait to see you again. I knew I loved you and then it was confirmed for me 100% when I saw you. I can't wait to meet your son.*

Allen: *Me too. It's all I can think about. I know that my kid will love you just as much as I do. You are perfection, the total package, a trophy to be shown and proud of. To say you're hot would be an insult. You are beautiful in every way. Now that we know it's real, you have to work on your end of the…. situation. I won't be played for a chump. If you do love me and want to keep me, you need to do some decision making. This isn't a game and it's not a fairy tale. If your husband makes you happy, I'm outski, but if you want me—do the work. Text me when it's ok to text back. I love you gorgeous.*

I read the messages repeatedly, until the words blurred through my tears. My mind raced to try to think of something, anything to make this look different from what it obviously was. She knew when she asked me to come with her that I would say no.

That's why she made it so easy for me. We had never taken separate getaways before; all of our vacations were always taken together. She had changed. She was… happy, and now I knew that it was because of HIM.

She had healed alright, healed herself right into someone else's family. She reacts like I say the word abortion instead of adoption and now she can't wait to meet HIS son?! This is too much. She had thought that I wouldn't understand her healing process, and she was fucking right. There was nothing to make me understand this. When was she going to tell me? WAS she going to tell me? Would I just have come home one day to a note saying adios Aaron, it's been fun?

I raced to the trash can and threw up, my love turning to bile in my throat and spewing out. All her words, all of the love, all of the plans and promises turned to poison in my heart. Every memory a lie, every struggle un-felt by her. Did she even want children with me? Did she ever love me? What was the point of all of this? Every single question branched off into five more questions, attacking my mind like a murder of crows.

I lit a cigarette on the way to my car., drove to the corner store and bought a LOT of beer. I never drank, but if there was ever a time for it, now was that time. I chugged one in the parking lot and opened another for the ride home. My father always said that the road to a man's self-destruction always began with a woman. *It looked like he was right,* I thought as I threw a crushed can out of the window. I lit another cigarette as I pulled into the driveway and saw her car there. Without thought or care, I drank two more before going inside, lit cigarette and all.

She was sitting there on our bed with her phone lying in front of her with the screen lit up. Her eyes widened when she saw me smoking in the house. She opened her mouth to say something about it but then quickly closed it, realizing the shots weren't hers to call here. She wasn't upset or crying. She just looked numb.

I've never wanted to hit a woman in my life, but my hand throbbed with the desire to. I rubbed my hand on my jeans to try to disperse the energy.

I loomed over her and cried, "You can tell Allen that it's safe for him to message you now. He can message you any time he wants, and it's not my problem anymore. You've never been who I thought you were. The past 8 years were all a lie!" I said as my words turned to blubbering tears. I didn't want to give her the satisfaction of seeing my heartbreak, but I couldn't help it. Through all my anger and all of my hate, I still saw her there sitting on the bed. She looked so small and lost. All I wanted to do was hold her. That wouldn't happen though, not ever again if I could help it.

She finally cried and apologized. She promised that she would end it and block him and get rid of social media entirely to work on us. She said she wanted to be a better wife and got lost. She said she got mixed up, and the situation became too big for her to get out of. She needed help. She actually had the gall to tell me that she was glad she got caught and now I could help her get out of it.

She said she never stopped loving me and never loved him.

"I felt neglected by you, Aaron! I felt like I lost you and myself when we couldn't have kids! I thought I had found myself and figured out life, but I was wrong. I went to leave you and I couldn't do it. Aaron, I will do anything to fix this. We can come out of this stronger and with a better understanding of each other."

We spent an entire week apart, me taking a trip of my own out of state to clear my head. She went to my parents and cried to them about what she had done. She apologized for hurting their son and asked for their forgiveness, figuring it would eventually lead to mine. Though manipulative and inconsiderate to my parent's mental health, it worked. She picked me up from the airport and again I hugged her so hard I lifted her off the ground.

We went home and reconnected. We really talked. For hours into the night and then again when we woke up the next day. We had worked a lot out and decided what we needed from each other to get past this and not let it ruin us. The only thing I asked of her was to block his number from her phone and to never, under any circumstances, positive or negative, have contact with him again. This was MY time to heal, and that was the only way I was going to be able to do it. I wouldn't forgive her twice.

Though I didn't tell her at the time, she did ruin us. I saw Allen's picture next to his messages, so I knew his face. Every time I would go to kiss her or touch her, I would see his face, like a ghost. Allen making her laugh, him kissing her forehead, him making her sweat. I hated it. I wanted to hate her, but I couldn't. Despite everything, she was still the woman I loved and always would be, even if I did leave her. We would get through this. A part of me already died when I found out what she did. Maybe that part will grow back stronger. Better.

A few more months went by, Valentine's Day came and went with no issue. I was nervous about it, but Katie tried her best to make sure it was a good day for me, for us. I started to see the ghost of Allen less and less. Katie was turning into the woman I married again. It was terrible that she needed this to get back to that, but as long as I had her, we could work it out. She would never leave me again, she promised.

She had deleted social media as promised, and Allen's number remained blocked. My heart started to slowly heal. I was well on my way in love with her again. Not like nothing happened, but like we didn't let it break us. I stopped checking up on her as much. She felt terrible about it and seemed to punish herself more any day than I ever could. So, we let it fade into the past. She'd never leave me again, she promised.

"Hey, Aaron, can you please look at my phone? I think I have some sort of virus," she asked me, concerned. I laughed at her and joked, "You know how you get that don't you? Too much freaky peeky. What kind of sick shit have you been looking up?"

She slapped at my arm, giggling on her way to our kitchen. "Nooo. Come on, I can't get any of my pictures to load and I wanted to send some to my mom. You're off today, please?" I told her I would help her and to give me an hour with her phone. I would back up her pictures and factory reset if the problem was too bad.

I transferred her pictures over to our computer just in case. Then I unplugged her phone and looked through her messages to make sure she didn't lose any important numbers or pictures if I reset it. I went to the text settings to see if there were any locked or starred messages with pictures of us. I saw an option on the phone that said blocked messages. With very wary but overwhelming curiosity, I opened the folder.

There were so many, all from Allen.

Haven't heard from you. I'm sorry about how I act sometimes. You know I love you. I just think that when two people want to be together that they should do anything they can to do so. It's hard for me to imagine the situation you are in at home and I just get frustrated. Tell me you are thinking of me. I love you toots.

I am so lucky to have you. I thought of you last night before going to bed but that's nothing new. You know how hard you make me.

Just want you to know that no matter how mad I get at you I could never stop loving you, and I'll never turn my back on you.

You look beautiful today

I love talking to you. It's been the best part of my day for months

Good morning! You are rockin' it today babe.

They went on and on like that and my mind snapped. The frail bandages holding my fragile heart and mentality all fell away. I looked over to her across the room. My breath was coming out in faster and bigger huffs and my face was burning red.

She looked at me, confused. "Wha?" Before she finished her word, I was out of my chair and in front of her. "The time for words has ended now. I only asked you for one thing... Just one fucking thing." I stood up to leave and she launched up from the couch, throwing herself on me.

"Aaron, please. I don't understand. We have come so far, and I've worked so hard. Why would I do that just to talk to him again? I haven't been talking to him! Don't go anywhere. I know I fucked up last year, but I wouldn't do that again." Her sobs grew louder.

No way, there is no way that she gets to be the one to cry here. She doesn't get to feel anything but shame right now. I'm the one who should be crying, but of course everything was always about her. I can't even have feelings without her trying to steal them so she could end up being the victim. I have to stop it, get her to be quiet. I slam my hand over her mouth, but she still sobbed, soaking my hand in snot and tears. Her wails grow louder and louder, repeating the same words over and over. It's as if she thought the more she said them the more I would have believed her. The only things that I do believe are that I can't bounce back from this twice. I can't live with her, and I can't live without her, as the saying goes.

My hand dropped from her mouth to her throat, the other coming up to meet it. Now it was my turn to feel. I cried and sobbed as I squeezed my hands tighter... and tighter. Fragmented wedding vows grunted out through my teeth as I heaved with tears. I wanted my face to be the last thing she saw as the life faded out of her eyes.

Her wails turned to whimpers until finally barely any sound could escape at all. Till death do us part, my darling, and I promise I won't be far behind.

So, this is how we got here, my mother-in-law's voice on the home answering machine. Her daughter turning colder by the minute on the floor. My hands shaking and my sides sore from the sobs. The light of my life is gone. Why did she have to do this to us again? She always said she was born to be my wife, and that she would die for me. Well, here we are. She ended up being true to her word in one sense at least through all of this.

I checked the block list again and see a new message from 18 minutes ago. *I love the way you smell.* It read. Enough of this shit.

I hit the call button on the message. It rings and rings until finally a woman picks up. Before I have any room to say anything, she starts yelling at me.

"You have to be some kind of stupid to continue to call after all that you've done, Katie." The woman said my wife's name as if it was disgusting on her tongue. She continues, "As far as his son and I are concerned, you might as well have been driving the car that killed him. Do you know he had messages set up prescheduled to send to you for two months? It's nice to know YOU have messages from him after he's dead, but what about his son?! You heartless slut!"

She's going on and on, hysterical with fury. I tune her out and hang up the phone without a word. I think, really think about what she has said. She said the words 'killed' and 'prescheduled messages'. Katie was telling the truth; she hadn't contacted him. This also explained why he still went on as if they were together. It really was over; she really was mine again. Oh, my god, I've killed her!

I run to the bathroom, rifle through the medicine cabinet, and grab a bottle. I don't plan to call the police or turn myself in. Surely the neighbors heard the noise and called them already anyway. I don't know if I will have the courage to take the contents of this bottle.

For now, I'm going to snuggle up to my sweetheart. I will hold her for as long as I can and not let go. I hold her and smell her hair as I wait for the knock to come at the door. They can try, but I'll never let her go. She will never leave me again, she promised.

Till death do us part, sweetheart.

THE QUIET HOSTS

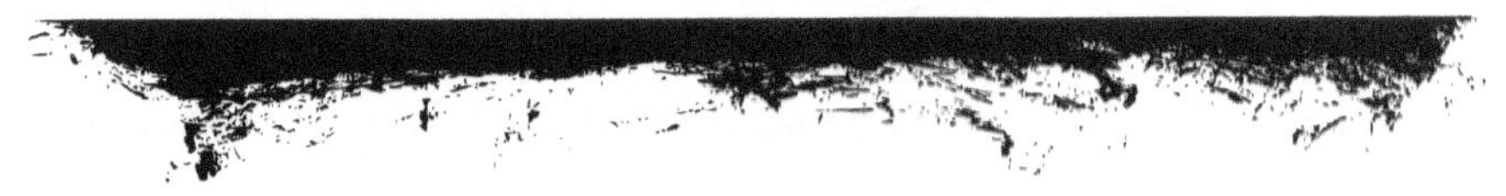

Today is day two since my wisdom tooth extraction. The throbbing is so much worse today than it was yesterday. Every single sound seems to agonizingly resonate throughout my jaw; *drip... drip... drip*. Oh, my godddddddd; that sound makes me want to ram my head through the wall.

I've recently discovered a small hole in the ceiling of my bathroom. There must be a weak spot in the roof that collected water over time, ultimately breaking through the ceiling's drywall.

I hadn't found it till I slipped on a wet tile and almost went ass over teakettle in my bathroom last night. The pain medicine and my general state of grogginess didn't help things either.

My mouth tastes absolutely awful. I fell asleep with it open and apparently hadn't closed it all night. Struggling to find my equilibrium, I roll over and spit. Nothing comes out, I might as well be blowing dust. I trudge through the path to my kitchen as if wading through quicksand. Each step is slow and sluggish with effort.

The pain in my jaw is maddening. All I want to do is smoke a cigarette to get some kind of relief! Something to help me gather the mental fortitude to deal with this constant ache.

In retrospect, it seems like all I've been doing for the past forty-eight hours is sleeping. I walk back towards my bed, though.

My throat is brought back from its desert death by a chugged bottle of water.

I am almost to my pillow when I see a dark, squiggly line jump out against the contrast of my pale pillowcase. I spring away quickly and turn on the light. Laying on my pillow is half of a centipede, still wriggling and flailing each of its legs. I loathe centipedes... are they even necessary to our ecosystem at all? People say everything has a purpose.

How is it even moving after it's been severed? More importantly, where's the other half? This is insanely grotesque and unnerving, even for a man of my age. I wrap my hand in toilet paper, stick it inside of a Ziploc bag, and then grab the... remains and give them a burial at sea.

I am exhausted from the consuming aftermath of adrenaline and panic. The bedding is searched twice, changed out, then searched again before I can find the comfort to lay back down. A deep but fitful sleep soon greets me.

Over the coming few days, the pain in my jaw has eased a little. I can't tell if it's a sign of healing or if I'm just somehow getting used to the pain. The fog hanging over my existence lifts, and I decide to indulge in a hot shower.

The almost unbearably hot water is a jarring but soothing relief to my senses. My hands are halfway through sloughing the rest of the soap out of my hair when I am incapacitated by a blinding pain in my left ear. I don't understand how I keep reaching these new levels of Hell.

Before this moment, I was sure that tooth pain was the most mentally unnerving to experience. Now I know that I was wrong. The splitting pain of an earache can be just as devastating; more so if you factor in the equilibrium changes.

Why now? Hadn't I been through enough? I shudder after turning the water off to hear the drip... drip... drip of my ceiling into the bucket I had placed underneath.

I need to get it together so I can go up there and patch that hole before the damage gets any worse; sure, as hell can't afford to pay a roofer. Thankfully, I still have one day left before I have to go back to work.

Management arranged it to where I worked ten days in a row and then got to have off the day of the extraction plus four more after.

Just to be safe, I give the dentist's office a call and explain what's been going on. They told me that the lingering pain in my jaw is normal, but it shouldn't be affecting my ear. The pain in my ear spikes as she says this, almost feeling like a biting deep in the canal.

As horrifying as it is, I can't help but continue to obsess about the missing half of the centipede. My mind runs wild with the possible orifices of entry that are held within my body. There are my ears, my nose, my mouth, my eyes... those *unmentionable, unimaginable* places. Each option terrified me more than the last. My skin crawled with the thought of it... all those legs.

I can almost hear them skittering inside of my ear. Surely it can't have survived this long. The movement I saw had to have been leftover energy and muscle memory reactions to its severed body. It's not the brooms in Fantasia. It makes no biological sense to halve one into two and then have those two pieces morph into whole new creatures.

The urgent care clinic is open until five today. They must be able to do something about the needle-sharp pain in my ear. If there's anything living in there, it needs to come out... NOW.

My stomach heaves: the pressure of the tremor renews the agony in my jaw. The core of my mentality does battle tooth vs. ear. My foot rams down on the gas pedal in an attempt to quicken the route to Urgent Care.

I arrive to see two patients waiting inside before me. Both are sag eyed, noses aglow with the telltale redness of a cold virus. This is a good sign that the wait shouldn't be long at all. A gorgeous nurse emerged from a door that led back to the patient rooms.

She lightly clears her throat. "Kyle Galapon?" I rise to my feet in response. She smiles at me, shattering the illusion of beauty I found myself enchanted with not one minute ago.

"Right this way Hun. You're gonna be in room six. The nurse will be in soon to speak with you before the doctor comes," her crisp scrubs *swish* as she leaves the room. I explain my tooth and ear situation twice. Once to the nurse and then again to the doctor.

It's almost impossible not to jump as he sticks the Otoscope inside my ear. The chill of the plastic cover sears the inside of my head like a branding iron. "Ahhh... I see the problem here, pret-ty nasty." *Tsk.* The doctor shakes his head slightly.

My voice cuts through the tension in my heart like an axe. "What is it? Is there something in there? Get it out! What do you see in there?"

He places a hand on my shoulder to assuage my fears. "You don't have anything in there but fluid buildup, likely a result of your recent tooth extraction. That's a pretty serious infection you have going on in there. Let me look in your mouth."

I open my mouth widely so he can peer inside. "Bingo. There it is. It looks like you have a tiny abscess in your extraction site. I can see it clear as day. I'm gonna give you some antibiotics. That should help clear up both the abscess and the ear infection. Make a follow up appointment for two weeks from now on your way out."

The pharmacy close to my house is still open, so I get my prescription filled. I take the first opportunity available to swallow two of the antibiotics and continue my drive home.

Work will be here before I know it and I need to be ready. My girlfriend Penny from back in college had two wisdom teeth removed. She was back to laughing and kissing my ugly mug two days later. It's bullshit that it's taking me so long.

The next morning, I woke up at a new threshold of pain. The bathroom mirror shows the swelling of my jaw even through the skin. Unhinging my mouth like a snake, I lean in to inspect the inside of my mouth. I can see the bump pulsing, almost beckoning for me to pop it.

As gentle as I can manage, I place two fingers inside my mouth and give a small squeeze. I can feel the give of my flesh through the pain; like a strained knuckle begging to be cracked. Then, I feel something else, a jitter. It's slight and fleeting, but it was there. A sensation of shimmying, skittering creeps throughout my gumline.

With no more patience left and my fear rapidly building, I jam my eyes shut and squeeze for dear life. My mouth instantly fills with a foul, rotten paste. I spit into the sink and refuse to believe my eyes.

In my sink lay a few tiny, circular moving orbs. It doesn't take long to see what's causing their movement. Emerging from underneath the orbs lay two tiny centipedes, writhing... squirming with life.

How many more of them are in there?

CRICKET'S CURSE

"*Never kill a cricket in your house, lest your family member meet the same fate.*"

The carpet smells of decay and mud as I flatten my face against it in an attempt to hide under my wife and I's queen-sized bed.

An incessant banging at the door resonates through my brain, feeling like I'm being impaled with an iron spike. Each knock slams it deeper into my throbbing temples.

"Mr. Hutchinson? Are you home?" A voice inquires, yelling through the mail slot. I recognize it as my son's 2nd grade teacher, Mrs. Mason.

Dread grips my heart in cold, grey hands as I remember not closing the shade to the kids' bedroom window. I wonder if she can see the red painting the walls, turning brown over time with oxygenation. Undoubtedly, I decide.

"Joseph hasn't been to school for three days now." Mrs. Mason continues. "We've been trying to call you. Is everything alright? Mrs. Howell says Courtney hasn't been in either. Truancy is a profoundly serious issue in our district. I know I don't have to tell you that, Mr. Hutchinson. Please contact us."

Although irritating, the tone of her voice makes me thankful that she was Joseph's teacher. She spoke with the perfect combination of care and assertiveness; a difficult thing to do. I wonder if she spoke to her husband and colleagues the way she spoke to me just now; like a child reminded to put their shoes away after coming in from play.

Mrs. Howell was our daughter's fourth grade teacher. A memory flashes through my mind's eye of my wife Michele grabbing my hand as we were leaving the kid's school. We had just walked out of the double doors, tunneling through swarms of parents as everyone tried to get to the parking lot. It was 'Meet the Teacher Day', orientation. Michele grabbed me, eyes alight with the prospect of a happy future for our kids.

"Oh my god Jake, I love her," she beamed, relaxing her head against my chest. "I hope Joseph has her for fourth grade." My wife brought a hand up lovingly to my face as we watched our kids. Courtney was giggling with her friends as Joseph searched the flower beds for grasshoppers.

Not that any of it matters now.

Before I get too far ahead of myself, I want to explain. The medicine is starting to kick in and there's not much time. My family means more to me than anything else in life. That's exactly why I had to do what I did; to protect them.

It started when something crunched under my foot as it slipped out from under me. A smattering of legs, antennae and white goo left behind in its wake.

I wondered where its red blood was. Cockroaches, spiders, and all sorts of other bugs, save for ticks and female mosquitoes, left behind black or white sludge. I questioned whether or not their bodies contained blood like ours did. Maybe there was just too little of it to see with the plain, human eye.

Our son Joseph loved insects, grasshoppers especially. He must have brought one home, despite Michele and I's many lectures about not bringing any bugs home. He could touch them if they were safe, but he must always put them back where he found them. It disgusted my wife and I both, really. But kids will be kids. As long as he wasn't hurting anything, I figured what was the harm?

Horror takes hold of my senses as I realize what type of insect it is that I've just killed; not a grasshopper...but a cricket. My grandmother's words rang through my ears at a deafening volume. *"Never kill a cricket in your house, lest your family member meet the same fate."*

My breath hitched as I wrapped a wrinkled tissue around what was left of the creature to clean it off the floor. I remember feeling stupid for being frightened. I mean, it's not like I did it on purpose.

Michele and the kids were visiting her parents, who lived about three hours away. They left earlier that morning and planned to be back by the end of the day. I took the opportunity to stay behind and make some repairs around the house. It was a lot easier and faster to get things done without little ones under foot and Michele asking 'how much longer I was going to be' every ten minutes.

My hammer wasn't where it was supposed to be, causing me to have to drop what I was doing and travel out to my shed. It was a broken-down old thing. Years of laziness and mis-care led it to the dilapidated state it was in now, filled corner to corner with neglected and cast aside items.

The latest symptom of its failing form was a nickel-sized hole in the rear left corner of the roof. That, as luck would have it, just so happened to be directly above where my old toolbox was.

Rusted metal hinges creaked under the weight of the contents of the plastic box. I groaned as traces of water began to slosh out of the sides with each footstep towards the porch. *Great. I'd be lucky if anything in here was salvageable. That had to be at least two hundred dollars' worth of tools, if not more.*

A sea of black greeted me as I bent down and opened up the lid. It was a chirping, skittering swarm of crickets. Millions of hairs on hundreds of sets of legs rubbed in unison as their antennae twitched with feverish anticipation.

Cacophonies of chirps echoed through the late afternoon air as they exploded out of the toolbox. My arms swung frantically as they tried to invade my eyes, mouth, and ears. I would have screamed if I wasn't so afraid to expose my open mouth,

Tiny drops of rain had started to fall. I dashed in the house, leaving the rusted tools to be discarded once more for life's unexpected plans. Pieces of clothing were thrown off one by one on my way to the bathroom, my arms still swatting at imaginary prickles on my twitching skin.

Freshly showered, and cricket free, I poured myself the largest tumbler of whiskey that I could find. I'd done enough for one day. The shelving in the kitchen has needed to be fixed for over ten months now. What's one or two more in the grand scheme of things, right?

Television had always been an ultimate source of comfort to me. I turned it on and flipped through the channels; sipping my drink with annoyance at how late it was getting. It didn't do any good to get dinner started until I knew they were on their way. Michele hadn't called, so I assumed she hadn't left yet, let alone pick up something to eat on the way.

My impatience quickly turned into alarm as my eyes snapped open. It was pitch dark outside of our living room window. I'd fallen asleep in my chair, exhausted from the day's efforts, and lulled to sleep by the rain.

According to my phone, it was almost midnight. My family was supposed to be home hours ago. Calling my wife's phone was no use. I was instantly greeted with a full mailbox each time that I tried. When I called Michele's parents and woke them up, they told me she'd left hours ago but not to worry. She likely pulled over due to the storm. I looked outside; it was barely even raining anymore.

Again, my late grandmother's voice bellowed through my subconscious. *"Never kill a cricket in your house, lest your family member meet the same fate."*

It couldn't be. That's just an old schoolyard rhyme. The *'step on a crack, break your mother's back'* of my grandmother's generation.

Still though, superstitions had never proven me wrong. I walked under a ladder the day my dog Rocko was killed on the road. One time, I was playing baseball outside and threw the ball through the living room window. It shattered my mother's front mirror. Later that evening, dad's car got run over by an oncoming car. He survived, but medical bills haunted our family that took seven years to pay off.

The mental dam of my rationale began to crumble, letting streams of doubt and intrusive thoughts trickle in one by one. Just as the bands of hope holding me together were about to snap, the glow of headlights illuminated my surroundings from the front yard.

Courtney burst through the front door.

"Gotta pee!" She announced as she zipped past me into the dark house.

Michele trailed slowly behind her, holding a sleeping Joseph in her arms. Aggressive whispers left her lips, ordering Courtney to be quiet so she wouldn't wake her brother up. She looked weary, stressed even.

"Hey babe, love you. Get a juice cup ready in case he wakes up okay?" She asked, briefly planting a kiss on my cheek on the way to our son's room.

The moment he was settled, she leapt into my arms. "I'm so sorry we were late. My phone died and the charger cord I brought wasn't working. There was a terrible accident in front of us on the way home. The other vehicle missed us by inches. It was a miracle we managed to avoid getting hit."

I hugged her back tightly, thankful to have my wife and children home safe.

"That's why we were so late," she continued. "We stopped to give statements to the police. The driver of the car ahead of us didn't make it. Jake, we could have been-."

She didn't finish her sentence, just collapsed into my arms in a heap of tears, overwhelmed with exhaustion from the day's events. I offered her the rest of my whiskey and rubbed her back as she gulped it down.

A debilitating nightmare tortured me in my sleep. The kind that stays with your soul long after you've woken up. I remember entering the house alone in the middle of the night. Our living room was a sensory deprivation chamber of foreboding; black and soundless.

I stumbled blindly through my home, hands outstretched, desperately searching for something familiar. A single beam of light appeared under our children's bedroom door. I used that light as a beacon and made my way forward; towards light, towards hope, towards... my family.

A siren of chirps consumed the silent atmosphere the moment I opened their door. My wife and two children lay on the floor before me, slaughtered. Their lifeless bodies were bent at unnatural angles; eyes wide in shocked thousand-yard stares. Each mouth hung open, impossibly wide as crickets entered and exited them. All three sets of eyes rolled towards me as I started to scream. Their jaws began to open and close with each resounding chirp, still teaming with crickets.

I awoke with a start, sitting straight up in bed as I gasped for air. Michele lay beside me, sleeping peacefully, blissfully unaware of the horrors my mind had just witnessed. The hem of her nightgown jittered and danced in the still, breeze-less room. It wasn't until she absentmindedly slapped her leg that I saw a tiny black head appear from underneath. The cricket skittered over her skin, making its way over to me as I jumped out of our bed.

"Jake, what's wrong?" She mumbled groggily, rubbing the sleep from her golden eyes.

"There's a damn cricket in the bed. It was trying to get fresh with you under your nightgown." I feebly joked through terrified teeth.

To my utter revulsion, she simply plucked it off the bed, smashed it between her fingers and threw it across the room, wiping her hand clean on the side of the bedsheet. I didn't need to hear my grandmother's voice haunting me this time, I automatically said the words to myself internally. That's two now, dead. Sure, I may have killed some from the toolbox earlier, but that was *outside* the home.

A morbid thought flew in through the windows of my temporal lobe, clinging to the walls and spreading through all of my senses. Which one of them was I going to lose? Who would get to live and who would die?

Seeing as I was already up anyway, I decided to get up and check on Joseph and Courtney in their rooms. Their faces looked so angelic, so peaceful. I couldn't imagine one of them growing up without the other, couldn't imagine my life without either of them. Favoritism doesn't exist when it comes to losing a family member. I'd gladly sacrifice myself if I thought it would save them.

As I began to close the door, the sharp staccato of a cricket's chirp pricked the periphery of my hearing. When I swung it back open again, there was nothing but an eerie silence.

I shook the rotted roots of death from my mind in an attempt to snap out of my macabre mental state. The rest of my sleep was fleeting, but uneventful.

When I went to wake up the kids the next morning, I hesitated before opening their door. My ear pressed firmly against it as I listened for a cricket's call. After a few moments of silence, I entered their room. Courtney woke up right away, but Joseph didn't respond as I called his name.

He laid with his back to me, face smashed in the upper corner of his mattress.

"Yo, Joe!" I said to him, shaking his shoulders gently. "You gotta get up bud. It's time to get ready for school."

His skin was overwhelmingly warm, a human space heater just like his mother. It was hard to cuddle her at night in the summer months because her body radiated heat when she slept. I smiled thinking about that. Everyone says both of our kids look like me, but their personality and habits are all Michele's.

I rolled him over to wake him, falling to my knees in terror at what I saw. My mouth filled with saliva as it readied to empty the contents of my stomach. The skin on my arms was riddled with goose bumps, making me painfully aware of every hair. Joseph's mouth hung open in a silent scream as insects scurried in and out of his mouth. A baby cricket left his upper lip, making a pathway for his left nostril, and that's when I lost it.

Michele found me crouched on the floor screaming; the sheets of Joseph's mattress had been shredded by my own two hands. The kids were huddled together on Courtney's bed, crying in terror. I flew to my feet, instantly running to my son. I checked his eyes, ears, nose, and mouth for any sign of foreign object or parasite. Thankfully, there were none.

"I'm so sorry buddy." I cajoled him. "Daddy fell asleep on your floor and had a bad dream. I'm ok. Come here Courtney."

My little girl ran into my arms, drying her tears on my shirt sleeve. "Now my eye shadow is going to be ruined," she whined.

"Eye shadow?!?" I looked at my wife incredulously. The wry smile on her face let me know that this was something that had been going on for a while now. *When did my little girl get so big?*

"Go eat breakfast, kids. Then brush your teeth and get dressed," she instructed. They both ran to the kitchen to follow her request.

"What the hell was that about Jake? Are you alright?" Her amber eyes were wide with concern as she grabbed my face.

"Yeah. I'm sorry. I thought I saw a bug in Joe's bed." I ran a hand through my hair and tried to muster the most sheepish expression that I could manage. I didn't want her to think I was bat-shit crazy, though I certainly felt that way.

I drove to work in a haze, fully aware of what I was doing, but my mind was a million miles away. It seemed to take a third of the usual time to get to work. The air outside was thick and hot; I cringed as a grasshopper hopped across the pathway ahead. *For Christ's sake Jake, it's just a bug.* I chastised myself.

My supervisor grabbed me most of the way towards to end of my shift; telling me I had an important telephone call.

"Hello?" I answered.

"Jake..." my wife sobbed. "There was a school bus accident. No one will tell us anything officially, but I heard someone say the number 163. Some of the kids got really hurt."

"Alright honey, calm down and pray. Even if it's not our kids' bus, you need to pray. Call the school again, keep calling until you get through. The number for transportation is in my black address book in my nightstand. I'm leaving work now ok. I'll be right there." I assured her before hanging up the phone.

When I turned down our street, I saw two vans in front of my house. The top of Michele's head was visible above the second vehicle, and it was obvious that she was crying. Horror gripped my heart, slowing it to an almost lethal level by the thought of losing our children.

Tears filled my eyes unexpectedly as she came into my unobstructed view. Courtney and Joseph stood; their faces pinned to her chest as she held them close. Each wore a confused and annoyed expression on their face.

"It wasn't their bus!" She called out to me as soon as she saw my truck.

That night we ordered pizza, ate ice cream, and watched a family movie. We all lavished the time spent together, healthy and alive.

More nightmares plagued me throughout the next week, all representations of the death of a family member. Sometimes it was Joseph, sometimes Courtney, but always Michele. I saw her death in many scenarios, each more horrifying than the last. My family was cast in their own roles in the final destination movie inside of my head, and they had no idea. My family was dying more and more every single second of every single day, and I was powerless to stop it.

After three weeks of torture, medications, meditation, and alcohol; I was blessed with an epiphany. I *did* have the power to stop it. I was the *only* one with the power to save my family.

The chirp of a cricket reverberated through the dead of night as I entered my kids' room in a drunken stupor. A spatter of goo flew across the wall, signaled by the first cricket's call as I decimated it with my fly swatter. Another echoed through my brain as one fell to the floor in eternal slumber, never to be harmed by bad luck or superstitions again. The third brought a barrage of blows as my grandmother's voice echoed through my eardrums. *"Never kill a cricket in your house, lest your family member meet the same fate."* By the fourth chirp, it was all over. I was the only one left. Blood was... *everywhere*. As I looked at the fly swatter in my hand, I realized it wasn't a swatter at all, but a gore smeared hammer. There were no crickets, only bodies. I was alone to face the reality of what I'd done; what I thought I *had* to do.

That brings us to the present. There has been complete silence since they've all been gone. The void, the sheer emptiness of silence taunts me. I suppose eventually there will be the buzzing of flies. Whether I'll be alive long enough to hear it is another story. The addition of my body to the pile may very well be the one that attracts them, like buzzards to roadkill.

My ultimate plan is to join them. Guilt gnaws at my insides as my bloodied hands gather every prescription bottle that I can find. It doesn't seem fair that I get to peacefully fade from sleep to death when my family met such a gratuitously violent end.

The teacher or police will find us. I have no doubt that they'll be notified in the next day or two.

A metallic, bitter taste coats my tongue as I fill my mouth with pills; making sure to thank God for all of the good I've done and the Devil for all of the fun I've had. I know the weight of my actions will weigh against my damned soul when the time comes, and that's okay. Wherever I end up, I can rest easy knowing I did everything in my power to protect my family. Nothing bad can ever befall any of them again. Their souls ascended with innocence, free from harm... eternally safe.

TRUNKER'S TREAT

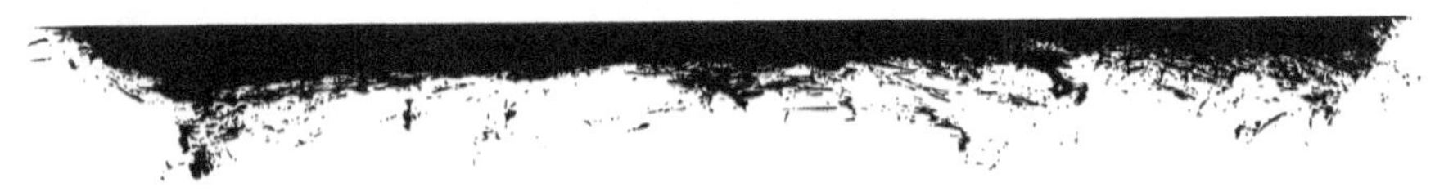

"I'm sorry Tony; I don't care what you have planned this year. Your little sister is six years old. Don't you remember how excited you were for trick or treating at that age?" My father couldn't hide the disdain in his voice.

"Yeah, but Dad... I'm not even going to be taking Bailey trick or treating! We're going to a large empty field with a bunch of cars with their trunks open. Can't you just buy her candy at the store? Why can't you take off, anyway?"

My dad rolls his eyes; real mature.

"Sure! Not a problem; I'll get right on that, dude. I'm glad that you think the work I do is so menial that I can take off at a moment's notice. It's not my fault they changed Halloween this year. It was October 31st my entire life and our father's life and my grandfather's before him. Why change it now? An entire petition wasted on stupid shit."

Now it was my turn to roll my eyes.

"Yeah Dad, I know... I've heard you go over this a million times. But I was supposed to go see Jade tonight, remember? It took me over two weeks to get the courage to ask her out. Now I have to cancel?"

A look of lost recognition crosses his weathered face.

"Bring her with you! I think it'll be nice! You two can't get into much trouble together with your sister there. Besides... I hear teenage boys who babysit their little sisters are all the rage right now."

"Dad, don't try to be cute. It's gross."

"Come on Tony please?" My father pleads. "Just help me out this one time. I know how important your friends are to you, but family comes first. Besides, there are supposed to be more cars than ever this year, seventeen."

Is that what she's been going on about? I've heard her practicing counting to twenty all week, I thought it was for school.

"Fine, I'll take her. No problem Dad." A wide smile forms on his smug face.

"Thank you! I love you. Besides, I don't think you're thinking of the big picture here."

I shrug my shoulders in response. He continues.

"With the trick-or-treating events being moved up this year, that frees up actual Halloween. Which, if you remember, I already took off in anticipation of taking Bailey myself. So, you help me out tonight, and on Halloween night you can do what you like, okay? I really have to get going now."

And out the door he went; only leaving the lingering scent of cigarettes and cheap cologne behind. How did I not expect this? Dad's become more dependent on me each year since our Mom died. I understand it's a lot for him to go through, but I lost Mom, too. I barely had a chance to mourn before he thrust me into her metaphorical footprints.

At the end of December, I'll be eighteen years old. There's only two and a half months left for him to prepare for life without me in the house. I worry about moving out and leaving him and Bailey alone, and that makes me resentful.

Anger boils through my brain that my Mom's gone. Anger boils through my blood as the drunk driver only saw fifteen days of jail time for killing her. The blood coursing through my heart boils because I had to stay behind to pick up the pieces.

It's like a mirror, sure if you break it once you will be able to put it back together. It won't look quite the same, but it's still a mirror. What if those same pieces were broken repeatedly though? Before long there's nothing left put together.

My inner rant is interrupted by the sound of footsteps skipping down the stairs. Bailey must be ready to go. I can't even remember what Mom said she'd be going as this year.

As much as it can be a pain in my ass, it ain't the kid's fault. I guess I should be stoked to spend a little time with her. She'll always remember this being the Halloween that her big brother took her trunk or treating. Hell, maybe we'll even go for ice cream after if there's time.

Bailey's smile had an effect on everyone that saw it. You know, contagious like a yawn. She looked so proud. Her costume this year, as I should have guessed, was a black cat, her favorite animal.

When she was about three, she heard our father talking to a friend of his about bringing in her black cat during Halloween because people like to be mean to them. I remember her asking me later that night why people would be mean to black kitties.

I explained to her that it was due to a silly superstition. People thought that black cats were evil and brought bad luck. She made up her mind then and there to make them her favorite animal. She said she just knew they weren't bad, just misunderstood.

Anyway, she's shaking like a rocket, about to take off into space with excitement. Her Peppa Pig pillowcase swayed back and forth, eagerly awaiting candy.

Jade texted me on the way out the door, asking how my day was. I told her all about Bailey and Trunk or Treat. She seemed really excited and invited herself to join us. Who would have thought? I gave her the location and time; then Bailey and I were on our way.

She hummed excitedly from the backseat for the entire ride. Only stopping to ask if I thought they would have this candy or that; excitedly saying that sometimes they give out stickers or erasers. A dry chuckle escapes my lips. When I was her age, stickers and erasers were considered duds. They were almost as bad as nickels or apples to us back then.

The lights in the field are all set up; it would be dark soon. There were lots of decorative booths and cars; each trunk had a different display inside. One even had dry ice coming from the back seat to make it look like a witch's cauldron; complete with a broom resting against the back fender.

Bailey was out of the car the second I had it in park, bouncing around the field with glee.

"Alright little one." I call after her. "Let's go to this first car."

She was fascinated. The backseat and trunk area were decorated with webbing. Two fuzzy, fake spiders sat in each corner of the trunk. A plastic bowl with spiders glued onto it was placed in the middle with any kind of candy you could think of inside.

Bailey gave the ritualistic trick-or-treat greeting and took exactly two pieces of candy. She even let out a little Mew when the car owner complemented her costume. It warmed my heart to see her enjoying herself.

Dad was right. There were exactly seventeen cars this year. If I would have let her, she would hit all of them in a little under ten minutes and it would be over. I told her that we should walk around between each one and see what else was there. We want to try to get the most out of our Halloween experience. She happily agrees upon spotting the Apple Bob station.

I tied up her hair as best I could with her wriggling around like a slippery eel. In no time at all, she raised her head from the bucket. Her mouth proudly displayed a shiny red apple in her teeth.

I congratulate her, place the apple in her pillowcase after drying it and we move on to the next trunk. This one has chrome baking sheets inside; each with various parts of a makeshift Frankenstein body.

"Tony!"

My head whips up as soon as I hear my name called. It was Jade! Out of all the girls in this entire field, she is the most beautiful by volumes. I can barely believe that she was there to see me and not someone else.

"Hey Tony! Are you guys having fun?" She leans down to be eye level with Bailey.

"Hey kiddo! My name is Jade, I'm friends with your sister. You look so amazing! I love your Peppa Pig pillowcase. Ask your mom where she got it, please. I want to get one just like it."

She throws me a wink as she says this.

Bailey murmurs in response, complementing the bracelet that Jade wore to be polite in return.

My devious brain has an idea.

"Bailey, I'll tell you what... why don't you hit those last three trunks over there. I'm going to stand here for a minute, okay? I'll only be ten feet away."

She did as I asked, looking back for reconfirmation as she reached the first trunk.

"Go ahead; get some good stuff!" Jade yells softly to Bailey.

"Thanks for letting me know about this Tony! It's nostalgic as fuck. I almost feel like a little kid again myself. Bailey's what, six... seven?"

"She's six." I told her.

Jade laughs. "When I was her age, I was Catwoman. Same basic concepts, I guess. I rocked it!"

She places her hand in mine. Her large, Bambi eyes melting my heart the more they look into mine. Out of all the girls that I have ever met in school, none have had quite an effect on me like Jade. She is absolutely perfect in the most imperfect of ways. The chicken pox scar above her right eyebrow drives me crazy.

It was stupid, I know that now. But in the moment, I couldn't help myself. I made my move, leaning in to give her a kiss that's only supposed to last for a second. My body's overwhelmed with heated tingles. That second turned into two, then into ten, till I got so wrapped up in her that I stopped counting. Still though, I know I couldn't have taken my eyes off of Bailey for any more than thirty seconds, if that. When the kiss ends, Jade's face holds an expression of concern mixed with horror.

"Tony... where's Bailey? I don't know what to look for because I've only seen her once; but I definitely don't see any black cats."

I turn around in a panic, my eyes scanning the lot as fast as quickly and carefully as possible. Jay was right here. Bailey is not here. I call her over and over, screaming for her at the top of my lungs.

"BAILEY???!? Where are you, kiddo?!?"

Jade calls as well. But there's no one there... not anymore. She turns to me once again, her face as white as whole milk.

Jade continued to stare at the emptying field.

"Tony, how many cars did you say there were supposed to be this year?"

"Seventeen." I reply. "I'm sure of it; Bailey wouldn't stop talking about it. She even focused on counting to twenty this week to make sure she didn't miss one."

We count the cars out loud together.

"One, two, three, four, five, six, seven, eight, nine, ten, eleven, twelve, thirteen, fourteen, fifteen... sixteen."

It being a community event made it almost impossible to find anyone of an official capacity. I have no idea who was in charge or who put the event together. When we finally find someone, we are informed that the seventeenth car had cancelled at the last moment. The field deputy looks annoyed behind his aviator glasses.

"I'm sorry, but in such a short notice, we weren't able to get a volunteer for the seventeenth car. Don't worry, we supplied the cars with extra candy to make up for the shortage."

Tobacco juice escapes from the left corner of his frowning mouth. He makes no attempt to wipe it away or spit it out.

"I'm sure she just ran off in one of the bounce houses."

Seventeen; I know I counted seventeen cars.

Where is it? And where... is Bailey?

DEATH AND OTHER INFIDELITIES

"**D**amn Pete!" My newest employee, Marlon, exclaims as he nods his head across the bar. "That woman's eyes are all *OVER* you. It's that time again, huh?"

I try to hide my devilish smirk as I give a nod of my own in agreement. I slide my hand down the side of my beer, using the condensation to loosen my wedding band. It pops off my finger and into my pocket effortlessly, as it has time and time before. My eyes take their time surveying the room before finally meeting her gaze. Jesus Christ, she's got gorgeous eyes. I've always loved redheads, but green eyes just take it over the fucking top.

"Oh my god..." Marlon continues, "Is that one of them Marilyn Monroe beauty marks?" Sure enough, right next to her left eye was the tiniest of moles, a period at the end of God's sentence. A vibrating sensation in my pocket interrupts me just as I'm about to walk over to her.

It's Maggie... my wife. *Can u plz bring home some dinner? Preferably something involving red meat. I've got the weakness today, bad.*

Fucking great. Putting all plans of an evening rendezvous aside, I texted back that it was no problem. I told her my phone was dying and that I'd be home as soon as I could. As soon as I put the phone in my pocket, our eyes met again. As if reading my mind, she smiled coyly and tips her head towards the back restrooms. I don't bother to tell Marlon where I'm going, just head on back.

By the time I reach the men's room, I'm already fully engorged in anticipation of what's to come. It doesn't take a genius to see what I just did there, by the way. Anyway, by the time I hear her heels click across the tile floor, I'm fully ready to go, all rationale leaving my mind as primal instinct takes over. She smiles and bites her lower lip at me; that's all it takes to let me know she wants the same thing.

***

By the time I get some steak at the store and arrive home, I pray Maggie is already asleep. My only desire is to go inside, change my clothes and fall into a sleep coma. That girl was a wildcat. She actually requested that I put my wedding ring back on before I gave her the best forty minutes of bliss she's probably had all month. These fuckin women these days...

To my relief, my wife's sleeping soundly curled up in a ball on my side of the bed. She always ends up sleeping on my side of the bed, holding my pillows if she goes to bed before I do. *Those nights seem more and more frequent lately,* I think to myself. Guilt creeps into my mind like a toxic fog momentarily before I shove it away. Maggie scoots her ass backwards until it finds my body. As I snuggle against the back of her body, she starts grinding her hips against me, a telltale sign that she's feeling good enough for sex. The sensation sends uncomfortable jolts through my groin, having well satiated its needs moments earlier.

"Baby, my boss was really a dick today, and I got pulled over on my way home. Can I just hold you tonight? Please?" I plead softly.

"Mmm-hmm," she murmurs, my words not fully sinking in. Her head shoots up seconds later, almost hitting my nose in the process. "What do you mean got pulled over?"

"It's ok honey. I was speeding a little to get home to you. He only gave me a warning." I lie smoothly. That seems to be enough for her because only moments later she's snoring again.

Two mornings later, I awoke to the smell of bacon and pancakes. Maggie limped into the bedroom, holding the food on a tray. She picked up the remote disgustedly and turned off a breaking news report on the television set. "Nothing but murder and madness," she muttered as she sat on the corner of my side of our bed.

She'd started having vision problems in her late teens. A few years after she married me in her mid-twenties, she'd started experiencing pins and needles in her legs and feet. One day we were walking in the supermarket and her leg just gave out, the muscle refusing to move.

We went to the doctor expecting a pinched nerve or at the very worst, neuropathy from unknown diabetes, which ran in her family. The MS diagnosis was one neither one of us saw coming, or even knew anything about. She had good days and bad days, but the doctors said the bad days would grow more frequent with age. That was ten years ago.

"Good morning sexy," she spoke. One of her sparkling eyes winking at me above a wide smile. Something was different about her, though I couldn't quite pinpoint exactly what. My wife straddled me over the bed sheet, and I could feel the heat of need radiate from between her legs.

"My my Maggie may." I teased. "Someone's feeling better today. Not that I'm complainin'."

She giggled adorably before leaning down to kiss me. When she did, I noticed something that's never been there before. "Maggie, honey, what's that by your eye? Did you hurt yourself?"

She climbed off me, plopped down on her side of the bed, and crossed her arms over herself protectively before placing a strand of hair behind a dainty ear so I could inspect it further. "What... this? I've always had this. I've never known if it's a mole or beauty mark, but either way I like it. We've talked about it before. Jesus Christ, what's with you?"

Needless to say, the mood ended there.

A few weeks later, I drove out of state for the weekend. The company I worked for was sending me to a seminar of a new piece of trial technological equipment that could *'change the way the World viewed plastic surgery'*. I made up my mind that I didn't give a shit about whatever it was they had to show me before the plane even landed. I was just grateful for the paid hotel and weekend. Maggie has become insufferably clingy in the past week or so and as hateful as it is to admit, I was glad to have the space.

"Are you sure you'll be alright?" I asked her for the fortieth time as I backed down the driveway. She nodded and waved me off, promising to have kisses and dinner when I got home.

I gassed up the car to take to the hotel, all expenses paid by the company, of course. My room was decent. The shower worked, and the bedding was nice. It even had free Wi-Fi and a continental breakfast. One thing I'd learned over the years of travel was that the nicer the hotel that they put you in, the more tedious and exhausting the event you were to attend would be. This was about a seven out of ten on the sleep in the rental car or being obnoxiously comfortable scale, meaning tomorrow should be bearable at best.

On the first day, they wanted us to attend a conference in the Hotel's main meeting hall before breaking for lunch. We were to be there from 8:30 AM until noon, a grueling three and a half hours of blathering bullshit. Once seated, it only took a few moments before I felt a pair of eyes burning into the seat of my pants. I turned around subtly to see a woman staring hungrily from behind me. It was obvious the only interest she had in the activity of the room was right below my belt buckle.

She was gorgeous. Once she stood, I was surprised to see that she was taller than me, a trait I normally stayed away from. Something about her smile though... there was the smallest gap between her front teeth that drove me crazy, a perfect imperfection that caught and kept my attention. We spent our lunch break up in my room, so wrapped up in each other physically that we were almost late for the second half. I didn't catch her name, and she certainly didn't care to know mine. It was perfect.

Maggie was waiting for me on the front porch as I pulled into the driveway. The way that she looked struck confusion and fire into my heart. My wife, who not even six months ago could barely stand without assistance, now looked every bit as good as she did on the day we got married. It wasn't until she began to walk towards me that I noticed the painful limp and weathered steps. "Hey Pete!" she waved proudly. "I'm glad you're home."

Even though I'm an asshole, I really do love my wife. It made me happy to see her and, in a way, at my darkest moments... after the sex has faded from the air and the bed is mine alone again, I did miss her. What kind of man would I be if I didn't?

Once again, something caught my eye that was slightly off about her appearance. My wife took me in her arms, and we swayed together to a silent tune. The smell of vanilla and roasted chicken melded wonderfully in the air as we walked inside. We continued to embrace as I nuzzled my nose behind her ear and whispered words of affection and praise. My movements sent a tickle throughout her shoulders, and she threw her head back in a loud laugh.

That's when I saw it. The hidden alteration that stood out to me earlier was now out in the open and screaming in my face.

Between her ruby red lips was a set of shining white teeth. Two of which, the front two, had the daintiest gap between them. Now I knew that certainly wasn't there before. I had a picture in my wallet to prove it. "My god love, are you alright?" I asked, slightly pulling away from her arms. "Did you get hurt? It looks like you chipped a front tooth?"

Her eyes widened in nonsensical disbelief as she thought over my question. "Shut the hell up Pete, you know I'm sensitive about my teeth," she stiffened in hurt and offense, disengaging from my arms completely.

I knew I shouldn't have. After everything Maggie's been through and all of the strange behavior lately, I knew continuing to spend time with other women was possibly the worst thing I could have done. But as you already know… that's exactly what I did.

An old friend named Carla from college had come to the next town over for the weekend and asked me to meet and catch up. She'd just found out her husband was cheating on her, the irony of that wasn't lost on me I assure you and wanted to come back to her hometown to clear her head and get some space.

I got a room a few miles away from where she was staying. We met up for breakfast and had coffee at a place I'd heard great things about but had never been to. She told me all about her marriage, the separation, and how she found out about the affair. In return, I told her about Maggie and how she got sick; along with the strange events that have been happening lately. I didn't delve too much into it, but I admitted things were off at home.

I'm not sure if it was the connection from our childhoods, back when things were uncomplicated and our hearts were light, or the unburdening conversation that led to more than coffee. We didn't have sex; in some ways it was worse than that. I followed her back to her motel room, we smoked a joint, held each other and cried. The red in our eyes was replaced with the color of tears as we talked about what could have been, divulging secrets too evil for our significant others.

Carla winced as I grabbed her hand, and I noticed a long, smooth scar across the top of her right hand. She explained she'd gotten it in a car accident, and the pain from the surgery flared up when the weather was exactly right. Our eyes met and lingered, bringing our faces dangerously close together. Our lips touched for the briefest of moments when all at once, a myriad of flashes played out like the screen of a television set. I yanked away from her, as if she was acid on my skin. Only it wasn't Carla. It was my wife's rotted, worm-eaten face.

Maggie laid pale in a hospital bed, a machine emitting whooshes and clicks as it did the job her lungs were no longer strong enough to do. I saw my tired form sit beside her in an old metal chair, the failing fluorescent lights flickering irritatingly against the yellow wallpaper. A doctor came into the room and said something to me that made me break into sobs. A piercing alarm rang throughout my ears as the machines declared her dead.

I stood at her funeral, silent and solemn as those around me recounted memories of good times together. Everyone commented on what a good wife she was, and how she loved her husband with all that she had. Each word of consolement turned rotten and the betrayal of my own actions stabbed through my back like a broadsword.

Out of the corner of my eye, I thought I saw her eyes pop open accusingly as they lowered her into the ground. My wife was terrified of fire and always made me promise not to have her cremated.

"I'm sorry," she started. "I guess I just wanted to hurt my husband like he hurt me."

"I should go home. It was really nice catching up with you. And if you don't mind me saying so, hopefully now you can see how sometimes good people get caught in bad situations. Stay in town, clear your head... *alone*," I emphasized. "Then, just when he can't stand it anymore, go home."

Maggie's cell phone rang unanswered as I drove the two hours it'd take to get home. I'd told her I'd be away for the weekend and after all the shit I've done to her, I was excited to surprise her by coming home early. If we could start over, maybe I could fix the fickleness of my soul. I always felt the need for *more*, never taking the time to stop and think to appreciate what I already had. Relief flooded me as I saw her car parked in its usual spot in our driveway. I wanted to see her, hold her, rediscover all the things I'd fallen in love with before it was too late. She'd been feeling better lately, but who knew how long that would last. Even at the most promising signs at the doctor's visits they still advised me to remain skeptical.

A putrid stench emanated from inside, assaulting my senses the moment Maggie opened our front door.

"Welcome home honey," she exclaimed through a radiant smile. "I've been looking forward to you coming home," her eyebrows arched as a look of lust overtook her eyes. She grabbed me by the waistband as she pulled me towards our bedroom. All signs of difficulty were absent from her steps. Hell, at the moment she was having an easier time walking than I was.

The smell intensified the further that we traveled into the house. Halfway to our room, I had to stop and cover my airways. "What the hell is that?" I gagged through muffled lips.

"The smell? I think a possum crawled up under the house and died. I haven't seen the trash bins knocked around in almost a week now," she remarked dismissively as she fought with the belt of my pants. "Maggie, STOP!" I shouted. She broke away from me like a wounded animal. Her bedroom eyes instantly replaced those of hurt and betrayal.

An unsettling silence settled over us as I took stock of the state of our home. Nothing looked moved around or emptied. The kitchen was clean, and the trash had been taken out. There wasn't even so much as a dirty dish in the sink. So why did it smell like a landfill in here?

Maggie was still silent, but hadn't given up on her attempt to usher me into the bedroom. She began to pull and paw at me relentlessly, like a feral cat trying desperately to avoid a bath. Now if this were an earlier time in my life, I would have welcomed this behavior, encouraged it even. It'd always bothered me how meek and mild my wife was when it came to intimacy and sex. But now, between the look in her eyes, the feeling in my gut and the smell in our house, it just wasn't happening. "Christ babygirl, what is with you?!? I just got home and want to relax for a bit. At least let me kick my shoes off. And for fuck's sake honey, I'm not gonna be able to keep in the mood with that smell. Like how can you stand it?!? I feel a migraine coming on and I haven't been home for fifteen min utes."

My breath hitched in my throat as my eyes landed on some-thing... not quite right. Just past my wife, two doors past our bed-room door, was our storage closet. I'd noticed that there was a foul colored liquid seeping out from underneath the doorway, pooling onto the tiles of our hallway floor. The middle of the door buckled and bowed against the weight of an unknown object. And I didn't need my gut to tell me it was something bad. I lowered my gaze to my wife's face, recognizing a look of terrified recognition as she looked behind her to the closet door. "Peter, no-" she started to yell, but I gently moved past her. "Please don't..." she pleaded from behind me through panicked sobs.

The door flew open the second I relieved the resistance from the doorknob. A stained suitcase falls flat at my feet, the smell multiplying tenfold and flying into my airways. I doubled over in terror and disgust and my mouth filled with spit. Bile crawled up my throat voraciously as more of the fetid liquid sloshed out upon impact with the floor, splattering on my shoes and the hem of my khakis. "What the fuck Maggie?" I asked breathlessly.

Only a number of things could have been held in that case, but I didn't have to guess. Some of the fluid had seeped through the fabric and the zipper track as well. The metal teeth of the zipper were stiff and marred with goo. A small section of teeth remained silver and untarnished, and between those teeth, was a strand of long, red hair. Not just one or two strands, an entire tendril's worth. "Wh—who?" I stammered. Maggie cut me off before hysteria had a true chance to set in.

"Who is she? Are you asking me who she is, Peter?!" I nodded my head numbly in response. "Well..." she chuckled maliciously. "You would know better than I would...wouldn't you dear?"

Shock robbed the breath from my lungs as I fully absorbed what she was saying. My mind instantly flashed to that night with

Marlon at the bar. Self-preservation overrode all worry of finding a body in my back closet. I held my hands up in defense. "Now honey… I dunno what you've heard but, I've always been a good man to you. You know you're the only honeypot I wanna visit."

She raised her hand slowly before landing a slap across my face. "STOP IT PETE," her angry voice growled through gritted teeth and tears of hate. "Just stop…" she continued, the torrent of rage having subsided a bit, giving her a chance to catch her breath and regroup a bit.

"Jesus Christ Margaret," I snapped. "You hunted some poor girl down in a fit of jealousy and killed her? How did you even have the time or strength to? I haven't said anything because I love you so much, but if you can commit murder, I think the time for mincing words has passed. You've basically been in death's waiting room for the past year. Now your health has returned to complete normalcy and you're killing people to boot. What the fuck is this? Give me one reason why I shouldn't call the police right now, you-"

"Love," she said meekly. "The reason is love." She took me by the hand, gently this time, and led me to the living room sofa. It was almost impossible to refrain from cringing at the feel of her touch. The same hands that ended someone's life were now trying to use *me* as a source of comfort. I had a really hard time coming to terms with that. How was I supposed to look at this woman the same way ever again after what she's done?

We sat down on opposite sides of the furniture as she began to speak. Her hands were shaking, so she clasped them together in her lap to keep composure. "First off, let me say that I know about the women. I don't suspect, I don't assume, and I'm not going off of the word of someone else… I KNOW. So, let's cut that charade right now shall we?" She stated matter-of-factly, her voice forceful but otherwise void of emotion.

"Pete when you asked me to marry you, I always knew there'd be a chance that your will power would let us down. You love me the best that you can and with all that you're capable of… but you're weak. You crave attention like your lungs crave air. When I got sick, I wasn't able to give you that attention anymore," her eyes filled with tears. I took my chance to speak as she paused to brush them away.

"Mags, you know I've never blamed you for getting sick. Please tell me you know that. I haven't been perfect, but I come home to YOU. I married YOU! But fuck, we have a rotting body lying in-" She held up her hand to silence me, and to be honest at that very moment... I was grateful for it. I didn't have to look hard to see the scar across her knuckles. My heart wrenched at Carla, the poor lost soul who would never go home to her husband.

Maggie interrupted my thoughts. "We'll get to that in a minute. It's not like she's going anywhere. Now back when I first got sick, didn't you say you'd give anything for a cure? For a way to have your wife back. Well, I caught you with your proverbial pants down. I'm not leaving you because of it and what's more, I'm healthy, Peter."

"Yeah, but how? How am I supposed to sleep at night knowing I'm cuddling up to a murderer? How do I know you won't try to kill me if I piss you off one day?"

"The same way I'm supposed to go on sleeping with your arms around me knowing that they've been around someone else! The man I married, the man who VOWED to be beside me in sickness and in health, died the day you stuck it in someone else. If anything, you started the killing first!" Her voice came out in booms, and the infliction in her words made it difficult to argue. She had me there. "We all are capable of doing things that we never thought we would. The human body and mind are the ultimate mystery."

Maggie stood up and walked over to our rolltop desk before opening the tophand drawer. She turned around with a letter pressed firmly to the skin of her forearm, wincing once she pressed hard enough to draw blood. "Oh my god, Maggie!" I shouted as I ran over to her. I understand that adultery is painful, but for her to kill herself over it was uncalled for. I won't lie and say avoiding the possibility of having to call the police to report two dead bodies didn't cross my mind either. I knocked the letter opener out of her right hand, ripping my shirt off in order to staunch the bleeding.

To my disbelief, there was none. The cut in her arm sealed closed, without so much as a scratch left behind. It looked like she'd gotten a dab of red watercolors on her pale skin. It wiped away like it was nothing, leaving flawless flesh laying underneath. "They give me life."

"Life?!? Who? What the hell is going on here?" I demanded; my mind was not able to absorb the events around me.

"The women that you put your love into. I find them, and I take it back. Their last breaths contain all of the energy that I need to heal. Little by little, I've been getting my life back. I was able to get the other women alone, using your phone to lure them to isolated locations. Don't bother to check your phone," she remarked snidely. "You won't find any of them. So, I guess if you wanna call the police go ahead, but it's not gonna look too good for you buddy." A triumphant smirk settled on her shiny red lips.

"Then, why is that one here?"

She walked past me to the hallway before giving the suitcase a kick with the side of her foot. "This one," she grimaced, kicking the suitcase again, much harder this time. "This one... came here looking for you. You don't shit where you eat Peter. And if I'm going to sit home and play the fool, the least you could have done is be discreet about your address. Boy was she surprised when I answered the door. By the time she saw our wedding photos and bolted for the door, I already had the knife."

My mind reeled at so much information at once. None of it made any sense, the feelings and emotions were all so multifaceted. What was I supposed to do? Call the police to turn in the woman I love for a crime I'd ultimately be accused of in the long run? But how could I live with her after this? Adultery and murder are two different things.

"Maggie," I said softly. "Baby, I am so sorry. None of this is okay. We've got to get this out of the house. It's not safe or healthy." The irony of being worried about the rotting life my wife stole away affecting her air quality seemed so selfish and wrong. "Please. I'm so sorry that I hurt you. I'm not dead sweetheart, I'm right here! And I'll never disrespect you or be unfaithful again." I grabbed her in my arms and clutched the top of her head to my chest. She shoved me away violently, as if revolted by the sensation of my touch.

"Oh, but you will Peter. You will be unfaithful again, and you will do it soon. My transformation is not yet complete."

SOMNOLENCE QUANDARY

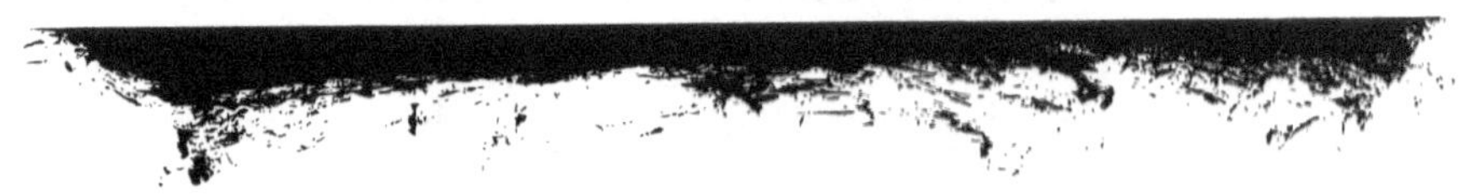

Have you ever felt so tired that it tested the limits of your very sanity? The type of utter exhaustion that made you want to revert back to toddler years and throw a screaming tantrum until someone directs you to the closest bed? No? Oh, maybe it's just me then.

I gave birth to my second child a couple of weeks ago. It's taking me more effort to get into the swing of things than it did with our first. The transition of caring for one child to caring for two is astounding! It is the most exhausting, mind melting, soul sucking, time thieving... heartwarming, pride swelling, and the most beautiful task to undertake at once.

Things wouldn't be so bad if I wasn't always so damned tired! My husband David tries his best but when it comes to nursing, there isn't much he can do to help. He goes out of his way to spend quality time with our other daughter, Haven, but I know she misses her mom. I miss her too...so much.

We used to do so many things together. We would make our own face mask out of smoothies. I'd give us matching pedicures; her little four-year-old feet mirroring mine as our toes dried in the sun. The endless paper bag and sock puppet shows... Those treasured moments almost seem like a lifetime ago.

I am but an animated, milk filled puke rag. This is my life now, and I accept that. Things won't always be this way. Before long, baby Kya will be the same age as Haven, and these fleeting memories will be long behind me. I know I'll long for them once they're gone. It still doesn't help with the exhaustion which takes place during every moment and memory made right now.

Today's been one fuck of a day, I won't sugarcoat it. However, I do apologize for all of the complaining. David went back to work today. I knew the day was coming even before I gave birth, but the knowledge didn't prove helpful to me at all now that today is that day. My smile and kiss goodbye are as genuine as I can possibly manage, and I hold in the tears until I'm sure that he's gone.

While running Haven's bath, she got into the fridge. She proceeds to pull out the largest jar of pickles we own and takes them out one by one to line up on the floor, juice and all. I start to fuss at her for making such a senseless mess when her mouth opens almost to the point of unhinging at the jaws. This was a sign of a sure meltdown; I knew the drill by now. Haven emits this head splitting scream that naturally wakes Kya up.

Many messes, kissed cheeks, and hugs later; Haven is in bed asleep. I'm trying to put Kya down after her feeding, albeit unsuccessfully. I'm not a new mother, I've done this before! Why is it so hard for me this time? My eyes feel like burning orbs if I keep them open and I don't dare close them for I'll surely fall asleep.

Absorbed in my own thoughts, I almost don't notice that Kya has fallen silent. I check on her; she's finally accepted the warm arms of slumber. My own selfish desires begin to take hold. I can smoke one quick cigarette, wash up and have time to sleep before she wakes up again for a night feeding.

I know that no one can hear me, and that's fine. It just means I can say whatever I want. The night air never betrays my secrets, and it always listens with a soothing ear. Calling David for a quick pep talk was out.

First off, he's working, but secondly, he isn't always the most sympathetic listener. The most I'd get is a "Well sweetheart, you need to buck up! You wanted to have more babies; I gave you more babies. Enjoy them! This is what you've dreamed of. You know how this goes… I work, you manage the kids and home. Just manage your time better." Nothing pissed me off more than these words, if I'm honest. Don't give someone advice on something that you haven't attempted to do yourself.

I tiptoe outside to my patio and light up, keeping the door cracked. The night sky is utterly gorgeous, and the air feels so cool. My eyes close with the first drag and I lean back, welcoming the peaceful atmosphere. A smile just begins to form on my lips when I'm startled by Kya's shrill cries. *"Oh my god baby, Mommy has nothing left to give you! I'm dried up! Tapped out!"* I say in a voice as soothing as I can manage. It's no use. My frame sags and I give way to a crying fit. I drop to my knees and run my hands up my face to my hair, slicking it with tears. *'I can't do this! I am so tired!'*

David gets to leave the house, be among other adults, take *a piss* when he wants to. These are luxuries I know I'll soon not get to enjoy—but, that's fine. David's right, this IS what I wanted. I just need to get my own groove going. Things will run smoother after that. Kya will sleep more once she gets older. My body is screaming at me to sleep, my soul aches with the need. She continues to wail as I continue to lose my shit. My bleary eyes look towards the sky in desperation, even though I know it holds no answers for me.

The sky is speckled with stars, the moon half full and bright. Something in my periphery caught my attention… a streak. It's a shooting star! I've never seen one before! Even through my exhausted vision, it's absolutely mesmerizing! A celestial body of pure white en-robed in green and purple trails, unlike anything I'd ever witnessed. It moves so fast; I barely have time to get my wish out into the ether. "I… I'm tired… Oh Lord, I'm so tired. Please… let me get some rest. That's all I wish for. I just want some rest."

I hurry the rest of my tantrum on its way and then head inside to tend to Kya. The rest of our first month home progresses along these same lines. I still haven't found my groove but am getting there. Whatever inner resolve I have managed to muster since becoming a mother of two girls isn't nearly enough for the sickness that is ravaging the inhabitants of our house right now: influenza type A.

David has called off work due to him being sick and also to help with our two girls. Haven seems to have come down with the worst of it. Kya hasn't gotten too bad yet thankfully, yay breastfeeding! I, however, feel like a living suppository from the devil's rectum. Thank Christ that David's here with us.

I give him a crusty lipped kiss, hand Kya over and head to our room for a much-needed nap. Sleep isn't kind to me. It's a fitful, restless sleep... the kind where you wake up and the bed's drenched in sweat. Your body's entangled in the sopping covers, and it feels like you're suffocating. When I finally do wake from my torturous slumber, I find that it's completely dark outside. The clock on the oven reads 8:39 pm; it was *11:32 am* when I laid down today!

"Hi Honey! Feeling any better from your nap?" David inquiries from the living room. "Actually, I hate to say it, but no, not at all." His eyebrows raise in protest. I finish before he has a chance to interrupt. "Please don't get offended... thank you SO much for my break today. I needed the rest. I don't understand why I feel worse now than I did this morning, more tired even. Do you feel any better, babe? How are the girls? I didn't hear Kya one time."

After informing me that he's feeling better and assuring me the girls are fine, I take a shower and then head back to bed. There's so much that needs to be done. The laundry from us all being sick by itself is astronomical. Each item of soiled clothing is like a horny rabbit awaiting a mate. Before you know it there's a laundry pile in every corner of the house. It can all go to Hell till tomorrow. I don't have the energy tonight.

A hand grabs my shoulder and aggressively shakes me awake. "What the hell Laura! I've been calling you for over an hour!" I hear David shout. Oh crapppppp. My head feels like death. My fingers slide down my face, stretching the skin of my mouth with a groan in an attempt to achieve some kind of clarity.

"David, what's wrong? What time is it?" I look at my phone and see that I have fourteen missed calls, four voicemails, and five text messages. All an even mixture from the school, my mother-in-law, and David.

He's standing there holding Kya, his free hand linked in Haven's. She's been crying. "Haven, sweetheart, what's the matter? Tell Mama what happened."

David answered for her. "You didn't pick her up from Pre-K today. Her teacher sat at that school with her for over two goddamned hours. I had to leave work! Do you realize how much you scared her? She thought something really bad happened to you! Not to mention you didn't pick up Kya from my mother's. You know Dad has the truck at work today and that you needed to pick her up. I know you haven't been feeling well, Laura, but these are things that can't ever be ignored, no matter what's going on. We aren't the kind of parents who forget their kids!" His tone softens as he sees tears cascade down my cheeks. "My god, have you been sleeping since I left for work this morning? Do you need to see a doctor?"

"David, I'm so sorry! Oh my god! I can't believe I did this! You know I'd never leave the girls except for today I mean. Oh Haven..." shuddering sobs cut off the rest of my sentence. How could this have happened? I don't understand... am I really that sick? Questions of sanity and self-doubt attack my brain like a fleet of fighter jets. I know there are lots of mothers out there who are worse than me, but it sure doesn't feel that way right now.

I've gotta get it together. No more self-pity, no more sleep. My kids need me. I go all out to make sure we all have a good day as a family. I want Haven to remember something else about this day, anything other than being forgotten at the school. She's only four. Maybe she won't remember this? Hopefully, it doesn't pop up in the recesses of her psyche as an adult. I made one mistake when she was four and she grew up to be a nihilist or something to that effect because of it. It's a thing, it happens.

It's thankfully a great but exhausting day, especially with me still getting over this death plague. The time for bed came and went for the girls. I walked out to the patio again to feel the cool air. I seem to draw strength from the sky at night. Maybe it's the moon? I'm not sure. The evening sky is vast and clear tonight. I can't help but wonder where my fallen star is right now.

David is about to lay down for bed. I'm very tired but don't want to sleep. Something that once brought me so much comfort is now evolving into a place of anxiety. I feel so drained. All the time now. I try my best not to be irritable, but I can be a right bitch honestly. My girls deserve better... my family deserves better. These are the last thoughts that run through my mind as I fade into a sleep that I know will not bring me true rest.

"Mommy! Mommies wake up!" My eyes snap open. My room looks different; I can't quite place it. Standing in front of me is my precious Haven. Except... her hair looks different. Her eyes... Haven's eyes are green, not blue. What in the living hell? "Haven? What did you do to your hair honey? It's so dark!" My little doll baby smiles at me with the sweetest face. "Mommy... you silly. It's me, Kya! Haven went to school today."

"No... no... Kya's a baby," her head cocks to one side and her smile falters. "You and Daddy say I'm a big girl now. I'm not a baby! I even go potty by myself now, bigggg poops," she giggles.

The corner of my eye shows me a taller girl walking down the hallway past my door. There's the same slight bounce in her step that Haven has. Shaky and not quite ready for an answer, I called out. "Haven! Is that you, babe?" The girl pauses and walks backwards to my room in a silly way. Haven's always been a silly child. "Hi mom. Before you ask yes, my homework's done. I got green today, of course, and we had pizza calzonettes for lunch with veggies. I did NOT eat my peas, sorry not sorry."

"That's good sweetie. Where's your Dad? Can you please get him for me? Take Kya with you, okay?" These two beautiful but alien children link hands and leave the room. I jump up and race over to my mirror. I don't look any different. Maybe a little worse for wear, but I just got over being sick. I was going to look a little sallow. My eyes darted around the room for my phone.

There's one lying on my bedside table, but it's not mine. I pick it up and swipe the screen to open it. Nothing happens. I tried several more times with the same result. I know it's not dead because the screen lights up. Frustrated and at my end, I rapidly start hitting the screen with my fingers. A juvenile effort, but one worthwhile. The screen opens.

According to the date on this lying piece of crap, it's three and a half years later than it should be. It doesn't make sense, *nonnne* of this makes any sense. I would remember the last three years of my life. Who the hell wouldn't? It's not like I got into an accident or had trauma to my head. Even with this time lapse, I know I'm not becoming demented so, what then? What explains this?

I need some rationality before I lose my shit.

The background home screen is me with the same two girls that I woke up to. The gallery is filled with photos that I have no recollection of. I'm in most of them, yet they're foreign to me. This slightly aged doppelganger family made happy memories and spent time together. It all looked amazing, but that's not us.

I had a baby less than a month ago. I still have milk, for God's sakes. Upon further inspection inspired by this thought, I am again proven wrong. No milk, nothing, like I never had children at all or had them years ago. My scar! The C-section scars! I roll up my shirt to reveal only a pink, multi textured line of flesh. It looked like it had been there for quite some time. What is this?!?

David walks into the room. Wow... is he losing his hair? *Not important Laura...* my mind snaps back to attention. My mind tends to linger on smaller details to try to avoid a bigger picture. A smile animates his face like it's any other day.

"Hey Sleepyhead. How ya feelin? You barely moved the entire night."

"David... I feel weird. Like I fell asleep and woke up in the Twilight Zone." I inform him as I try to rub my eyes free of this new reality. After he assures me, I always say that after a nap I continue. "No. It's different. I feel like the past three and a half years of my life are missing. The girls are so much older now. I don't remember that happening! Kya's just a baby!" My words begin to waver with tears.

There's a look on his face. At first, I mistook it for genuine concern, but I was mistaken. He pulls me into a hug and kisses the top of my head. "I know babe. They grow up so fast. I feel that way sometimes too; it seems like just the other day we were about to get married. Look at us now."

How can I make him understand what I mean? I tried a different approach. "How have I been acting? What did I do yesterday?" Now the mistaken concern earlier appears, maybe I'm getting somewhere. "Laura, are you alright? You've been fine. Yesterday was a normal day. You made pot roast for dinner, Haven helped you with the vegetables. I came home from work, you kissed me, the kids went to bed and so on. Just like always."

"Okay so I've been here? I'm like present? I haven't seemed distant or different or anything?" David takes my face in his hands. "Of course. Where else would you be? You're over tired, you've been taking too much on here at home. Get some sleep and I'll be in soon."

"David no! Sleep? I just woke up! The last thing I need is sleep. I never want to sleep again. I don't know how much time I'll lose! I can't afford to miss any more." I'm practically shouting at this point. He wears a look of total bewilderment. "Umm... yeah... okay, well, I'm gonna step out for a minute to check on the girls. You can take this time to kinda get it together a little bit ok? I love you; you're being weird," he begins to leave. "YOU'RE BEING WEIRD!" I shout back.

The day with my girls is magically mystifying but also overwhelming. I was expected to know everything about these girls. I wasn't doing a good job trying to pretend that I did. Time was going by too fast, before long it would be their bedtime. I decide to sit in their room and watch them sleep, I want to memorize every inch of their faces.

David comes in with a blanket and a glass of wine for me, which I gratefully accept. He's always known me so well; I wonder why he can't see that I'm utterly drowning right now? Before long, I can feel my eyelids become heavy with the weight of exhaustion. Try as I might to stay awake, I'm losing the fight. I don't want to sleep. I have to stay awake... have... to... stay... awake. I have to... st...

***

My subconscious is attacked by a much-unwelcomed dream. I'm standing in this vast plain at night, in the middle of nowhere, and there's a female figure with me. Her face is somehow unclear to me, but I can't avoid her eyes. Eyes full of green and purple hues just like the ones I saw following my wishing star. They look down upon me with a disdainful glare.

"I am she and she is me," she says with a snicker. "What the fuck is this, some kinda Dr. Seuss book? Who are you? What do you want with me? Why are we here?" She interrupts me. "Slow down and chill out, Jesus! I'll only tell you what your mind can handle, and you mustn't interrupt. I'm wasting my time here as it is. Got it?" I nod but there's anger in my heart, I'm sure it shows through my eyes.

"Good! I do what my kind has done for centuries, nothing more, nothing less. You asked me for rest, and I gave it to you. That's what you wanted, a break. You're welcome. That's all I'm sayin', I have to wake up now. Your girls are amazing and besides...

it's a Thursday. Thursday is waffle day; our favorite! Maybe I'll see ya again soon, maybe not, though. Enjoy your break!"

"WAIT!" She pauses. "Thursdays? Waffles? What do you know about my girls? I don't understand." I ask her. She lets out a long dramatic groan of impatience. "Siggghhhhh. What, do I have to explain every little thing to you? You wanted a break; you're getting one. Why isn't that sufficient? I AM SHE AND SHE IS ME. It took thirty-six hours to complete the initial transfer. When you're 'resting' I live on through your body. I get lonely and figure you're not using it, anyway, right? You're not even appreciative of the time you have with it. It's a toy that you didn't want until someone else started playing with it." A flash of her face is revealed and... I see a foreign version of myself. And with that... She was gone.

———

That was decades ago now. I've woken enough to be present a few times over the years to be with my family.

This time when I awoke, David was gone. He had passed away four years ago, and I hadn't been around for it, not the real me anyway.

My skin is thin and frail, speckled in aging bruises from bumps I don't remember. My chest feels thicker with each rise and descent of breath. There's a faint ringing in my ears and I cannot see across my room. I feel like I've been robbed... cheated. A moment of sheer weakness and desperation was warped and twisted against me. I'll never have my life back. I'll never have my memories. But she... will always be with me. I am She and She is Me. I hope I get to stay awake for the remainder of the moments that I have left.

REJECTED

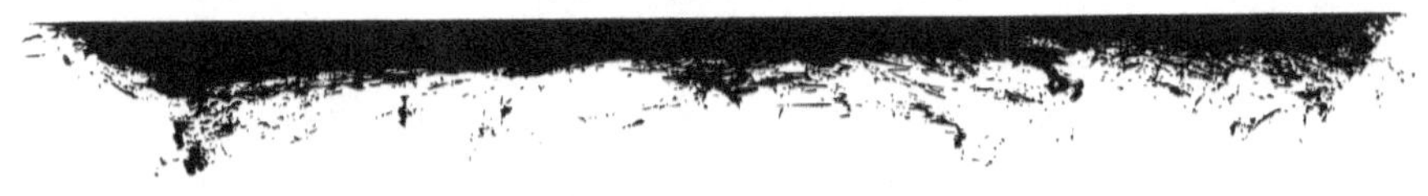

I want to tell you about my wife Gina, and some of the events that happened to us during the last week of her life. Told by a woman with a broken heart.

Gina pounded her brain as she sat at the computer. Her freshly dried nails rested above the keys, unmoving. There was nothing. Her mind was blank, completely blocked. This was the fourth night in a row she had dedicated herself to coming up with a great horror story; each night with the same result. She threw her hands up from the keyboard. "That's it!" She yelled. "I'm done!" She had a good run for a little while and it was awesome but now she was convinced that it was over.

My sweetheart had immersed herself in horror for as long as I could remember. I always told her that her rough childhood inspired her interest in it. It probably intrigued her to hear of people in situations much worse than her own. Even the ones that were obviously pure fiction, she loved them. The podcasts, true crime TV shows, the YouTube horror narrators, scary movies, Gina had done them all. Normally she was overflowing with ideas, but lately she'd just been completely tapped out.

She had had purely obsessive OCD for most of her adult life. Her therapist told her to start writing thoughts down during spikes. Well, one thing led to another, and before she knew it, she had her first story. We found her a writer's forum, submitted it and people actually liked it. Her second story turned out better than her first, and her third better than her second. It felt amazing to watch her creativity soar!

Gina got swept up in her newfound confidence. She sat at our computer for most of two days, typing out her heart and soul into a story. It was a common horror setting.

There were woods, a murderer, a sharp weapon, not unheard-of themes at all. It was all in the way that she told it and made it her own. Anything was possible for these characters once she started to write things down. When it was done, she was proud of herself and wanted to celebrate. We literally went out and bought a bottle of wine and some cigarettes, having not smoked in well over a year.

The next morning, a message got sent out saying that her story was rejected. I checked it before she did and was wary of how she'd react to it. She was slightly hungover and just a little bummed out. These things happen, and she had had a lot of positive reactions with the other projects she'd worked on. I could tell she was trying not to freak out about it.

Still though, four days later and she still hadn't been able to write a single damn thing. It was maddening to watch her go through. She had started doing this for therapeutic reasons and for fun. Now she was just putting pressure on herself and turning it into a source of stress. She always did this with everything good in her life, including us.

Things were quiet. She decided to take a break and smoke yet another cigarette. There were still quite a few left over from the other night, so I joined her. She put the chain lock on, let the door open a crack, and lit up. She hated how these smelled, hated how they made her hands smell. The porch light was off, the ember of our cigarettes the only glow in the night. She was starting to get tired. We would go to bed soon.

There were about five drags or so left of our cigarettes when we heard branches moving to the left of the house. We lived in the woods almost literally in the middle of nowhere. Cliche since she just wrote a story about this but, sometimes you write what you know, right?

She turned on the porch light so we could throw our butts out. When she did, her eyes got wider than I'd ever seen. She said through the lattice of the porch in the distance, she could see a pair of human eyes.

I quickly gasped, coughing on smoke inhaled the wrong way. My urge to slam the door was overwhelming. Instead, Gina gently turned the knob and closed it as softly as she could. Maybe if he didn't know that we knew he was there (assuming it was he) it would buy us more time to call the police. There was no good, decent reason why someone should be in our yard that late at night.

Gina was more than a little freaked out at this point. It looked like her mind was trying to break the fence of all the progress it had made so far. She was awash with every bad thing that could result from this situation, temporarily frozen by her thoughts. I grabbed her hand and rubbed my thumb over her knuckles. This always calmed her down. She had told me that more than once.

I told her to search for her phone. Of course, she couldn't fucking find it. Realization hit her like ice water poured down her back, her phone was in the car. She left it in there so she wouldn't be tempted to be distracted while writing. Mine had broken last week and wouldn't even turn on. We had no guns because, well, honestly, she didn't trust herself alone with them. So, she grabbed the largest knife we owned.

Knife in hand, Gina headed toward the window to look out at the yard when there was a bang on the door. We didn't answer, didn't move, didn't breathe. I didn't think that we even blinked, really.

Suddenly a gruff accent came through the door. "It's alright luv. I'm here to see Hannah." I looked through the peephole and saw a huge bloodshot blue eye staring back. I immediately jumped back. "Haaaaaannnnnnaaaahhhhhh" He called in a sinister sing-song voice.

Gina managed to pull together and pulled me aside to look for herself. The man was farther back this time, eyeing the structure of the door and surrounding windows. What the fuck?

He was wearing a Santa suit and was holding something behind his back. First off, it was the middle of April. Also, my girlfriend's name was Gina and mine was Savannah. Finally, she managed to somehow find her voice through her fear. "Y... you've got the wrong house," she said feebly through the door. No answer.

She took a peek out of the hole and there was no one there. Nothing but our porch, messy and exactly the way we had left it. I let a breath out in slight relief and ran my hands through her hair, pausing at the top of her head. Then the room filled with the terrible sound of twisting metal and tested glass.

He was trying to pull out our air conditioning unit from the window! I looked at her knife and then back at the ac unit. Any second the glass would break, and it would be ripped free. If there was a part of him accessible inside the house like his hand. Hell, even a finger she could've used the knife, but there wasn't.

Not knowing what else to do and quickly running out of time, we decided to run. I didn't like how our chances looked if we were to stay and wait for him to enter the house. Even with attacking him two on one. We had no idea what he was holding in his hidden hand.

Our feet couldn't move fast enough towards the back of the house. Her slender frame struggled to move the freezer while I tried to help her. She had insisted on placing it in front of the back door. Why she thought that was the best place to put it, I'll never know. She never thought we'd have had a probable murderer at the door with a machete or something either.

The back door faced out directly to the woods that lead out to a set of railroad tracks. I knew we could run along them until we got to the busy intersection a half a mile down. I could try to get help, call the police.

Just as she told me she heard glass breaking from the living room, the freezer moved out of the way. This also effectively blocked the path we had taken to the back door. The wind made a terrible howling sound through the broken window. I wrenched open the back door, stiff from years of inactivity. We jumped off of the porch, making sure that she jumped first.

We hit the ground running. My breath and heartbeat are deafeningly loud in my ears. This was turning out worse than anything Gina had ever thought to have written.

This certainly wasn't the thrill that she felt from hearing about or watching other people's horrors. She always said that a morbid, sick part of her would be excited that something actually terrifying was happening to her! Finally, something true for her to write about! She didn't look like she felt that way at all.

My sweet girl was trying to move as fast as she could while making as little noise as possible. Looking back toward the house, we didn't see any movement inside. My heart beat faster, and a chill ran down the sweat of my spine. She made good distance until, true to her horror stories, she tripped on a tree stump and went flying to the ground.

I saw her scramble to a crouch. I started to hear movement to the side of me. She didn't even have time to look around or scream, the man was only a few feet away from her. We had been tricked by him breaking the window and then coming around the back to wait for us to come out. Just like smoking out a foxhole.

Gina's mind refused to give up just yet. I saw her manage to get to her feet and get one step in before his hand clasped around her wrist. She yelped helplessly, wincing from pain and I think somewhat out of shock. "I've read all your stories luv," he said, leering at her.

His teeth were shiny and brown; like they were smeared with chocolate covered cherries. "And I've gotta say, this one's my favorite."

High above her head, I saw that he held a large metal ax. Its blade looked sharp enough to cut split ends. "No wait!" She pleaded with him. "You must have read it wrong. In my story the girl got away and survived. She made it to the railroad tracks." By now she was starting to cry, despite herself. "She made it to the railroad tracks," she shouted through sobs.

His smile got unnaturally wide on his face. The axe raised even higher, ready to make its fatal descent. "Oh no luv. Don't you remember?" He said with a laugh as the ax fell. "That story was rejected."

The space between us grew impossibly wide during our escape because of her fall. I was already en route to running back to her when all of this was happening. I screamed and shouted at him; in my frenzy I think I may have even told him to take me instead.

Love makes you do things like that sometimes; that's one of the ways you know it's real. I was too late. She's gone, and I'll never forgive myself. Sometimes, I wish that he would have killed me too.

DEADLY HOPES AND PROMISES

I just had to take time to tell you, my dearest friend, in case you didn't know. Anywhere that you call home, a piece of me will be with you when you go.

I closed out the message with tears in my eyes, setting my phone down to concentrate on the road.

Let's face it, the past three hundred and sixty-five days have been shit for a variety of reasons. It seems every family across America, hell... maybe even the world, has a horror story to tell. This is ours.

First, my husband fell from a ten-foot ladder at his framing job, completely shattering his left heel, foot, and ankle. Workman's Comp would have been fine, but we live in Colorado. Even with a medical card, if you fail a drug test for employment, that's it... sayonara paycheck. I always thought that was such bullshit. You mean to tell me that if Joe Schmuckatello doesn't pay attention to what he's doing and gets me hurt on the job, it's automatically my fault just because I enjoy a brownie or two after wo rk?

Fuck that, sir... or madam, can't be too flippant about that these days.

Anyway, that left me on my own to support us with my two bartending jobs. Which worked for a couple of months until all the bars were closed for safety measures. Yeah, I know I know. I'm not the only one who found themselves out of employment because of the virus. But Colorado is an expensive place to live. Even with Mark and I both working full time, we barely had money at the end of the week to go on a date or even make ends meet. It broke my heart to live in one of the most beautiful places in the entire United States but never be able to enjoy anything. All we had the time and money for was work.

Well, it was at this time that my best friend Maryanne started having troubles at home. We met in sixth grade when my family moved to Florida for my dad's work. I remember being not even a teenager yet and walking into that school for the first time. There were so many kids, all moving so fast. All their faces were so foreign and strange to me. Their mouths greeted me with welcoming smiles, but their eyes all told me they had other places to be and people they'd rather talk to.

Then I saw Maryanne. It was lunchtime, and I wasn't sure exactly where to sit. There was always a hierarchy with these things, and it was something I was beyond ill-prepared for. She flitted from table to table in a tight black shirt wearing the hugest jeans I had ever seen. JNCOs they were called. Her social graces came my way when she saw me sitting alone at a table. And our lives have never been the same since.

She was wild but smart, maintaining her grades just enough for her grandparents to approve of while trying to catch the eyes of any male in the 6th, 7th, or 8th grade. Thinking back on it, she had always wanted to be domesticated. When we moved onto high school and I began playing the field, Maryanne had always just stayed with one boy for a long time before moving onto someone else. We'd drifted apart slightly by then, but only socially. Our hearts remained with each other. Anyway, the point of this is, when I would tell her about a boy I had slept with, hoping to hear a story of her own, she never shared. I found out that this was because she had only slept with two people, and she had been with them for at least a year beforehand. I gawked at this, asking her if it was because she believed in all of the Catholic crap her parents had intravenously tried to feed her throughout her whole life.

But instead of getting defensive or offended, she smiled. "It's not that. I just don't want to fuck someone if I can't stand getting pregnant by them. If a mistake is going to happen, I'd better be able to look at their face for the next eighteen years." This baffled me. What she couldn't see was, in a way, I was right. While all of the other girls were laying on clinic tables and rushing to WalGreens for their Plan B tablets, Maryanne had mentally prepared for a family at a very young age. She always told me she'd wanted three kids, and well... she certainly got her way. Maryanne always did, you see.

It was no surprise that she got married at twenty years old, and before I knew it, I found myself in a delivery room at the local hospital, cracking jokes to ease her through labor pains with her first son. Although he could be controlling at times, Joey was good for her. If she demanded she tie herself to one person for eternity, I was glad it was him.

Months went by. I thankfully left our little town in Florida and made a life for myself in the outside world. Maryanne and I never lost contact, and through the years.

Maryanne and Joey had two more children, both little boys. I couldn't imagine how she did it.

As it turns out, she didn't... or at least she didn't think she could. I'd started receiving hysteric phone calls and social media messages from her, saying she was drowning in her own home and missed me. Well, Maryanne and Joey owned a large house on a huge piece of land and agreed to let us stay there free of charge. The timing was too perfect, and she had needed me as much as I needed her at that moment.

We arrived safely, completely unprepared for the heat or change in climate. It caused horrible agony to Mark's foot, which at this point after several surgeries was somewhat in working order. The jobs we had lined up had fallen through, forcing us to rely on standbys. I had thankfully gotten the job I had when I lived here at age twenty-one back and Joey got Mark hired on at a restaurant close to his work.

The first week was great, but what I had failed to realize was that I had outgrown the small-town feel of where I grew up, not to mention the people. My second day on the job I was putting in an order to the back kitchen. The customer requested that her dish come without peppers, so I called back the information to be helpful. One of the cooks pops his head up, stares me dead in the eyes and asks, "Just who the fuck are you?" It was obvious this asshole was having a bad day, or maybe just had a bad soul. Either way, I knew it wasn't my fault. As much as it hurt me at the time, if I didn't fire back a response to assert my dominance, I'd be dead meat. The kitchen would have their way with me every night that I served. I cleared my throat lightly, "Uhhh, Hi. My name is Michelle. I'm new here. Don't put peppers in that order. Nice to fucking meet you too bud." And I turned on my heel and left to check my tables. The moment I walked up to my next table, I felt all the color drain from my face. My heart began pounding, and it took all I could do now to throw up all over their table. It would be my first of many panic attacks.

I tried and left three different jobs due to debilitating panic attacks before I realized that my anxiety was from Florida in general. No matter where I worked, it would be the same. Meanwhile, back at home, the snow season had started, and our old managers were begging us to come back to work.

It took me two months of trying before I realized what I had to do. Maryanne and I were in the camper one evening folding my clothes. She would always sneak in while we were working to do our laundry and dishes. I think it was her way of begging us to stay.

She had Joey and the three boys, but she never really had anyone to talk to. You know, like *talk to talk to.* I couldn't imagine what that felt like. I was able to take comfort in the fact that my presence was helping her. But Florida was utterly eating me alive, heart, body, and soul. "Hey beebee where do I put this?" She asked, holding up a pile of crisply folded T-shirts.

"Lift the mattress, the area underneath is where we keep all of our clothes. Thank you again, you really don't have to do this." I smiled.

"Hush!" She snapped, but with a loving smile on her face.

I walked over to her, gently placing a hand on her shoulder. "So, you know I've been having problems lately right?" She froze for a minute, then nodded. "Well, I think Mark and I are going to try to go home next week. It's NOTHING with you or the boys, I've loved spending time with you. This just isn't home to me."

The minute I told her it was like a switch had flipped; I instantly felt like myself again. I could see by the look in her eyes right before she excused herself that I'd broken her heart. Maryanne had always tried to hide her feelings, but the message always got lost in translation, flooding her facial features with whatever emotion she was feeling. One of my favorite things about her was how expressive she was.

The tears betrayed her, sliding down her face despite her effort to hide them. I gathered her into my arms, giving her a long and needed hug.

It took her a little while to make peace with it. She wrote me poems, begging me to stay. There was an afternoon where we were slightly bitter with each other. She couldn't understand why I had to go, and it broke my heart that she couldn't see why I couldn't stay. Eventually we made up, as we always had done and would continue to do. We had decided to say goodbye the night before. She warned me that she wouldn't be home when we left to avoid an awkward goodbye.

The day came sooner than any of us had anticipated. As awful as it felt, the farther away we got from the Florida state line, the lighter my heart and spirit became. It was hard taking solace in something that broke someone's heart. But I had gone down there to help her, and not only failed at that, but lost myself in the process.

We pulled into an older gas station somewhere in Alabama, when I had a sudden burst of flirtatious spontaneity. Mark had been sexually neglected the last two weeks that we were there. He was too sweet to say anything, but I could tell he'd noticed. Who the hell wouldn't? So, with that in mind, I asked him to pull the truck to the back of the parking lot after we got done pumping gas.

With our combined mental exhaustion, the thrill of doing private things in a public place, and our newfound excitement for life, it was an amazing experience. I showed him all the enthusiasm that I had for his body and then some. Halfway through, a pop resounded from underneath us. "What the fuck was that?" I panted. "Did something break? Maybe a pipe got knocked out of place?" Whatever it was, we decided it could wait for a few minutes and didn't let it get in our way.

After we finished, Mark went outside to check the camper and truck while I got dressed and readied myself for the long ride home, barring no mechanical problems of course, knock on wood. I went into the bathroom to change, suddenly very self conscious of being naked in a strange parking lot. As I was pulling my pants on, I noticed a large bar of soap resting sideways on the floor. It was one that Maryanne had given me. My heart swelled, threatening to flood my mind with self doubt when I heard Mark come inside and close the door. "Okay. It all looks fine; we're all set."

"Yeah, I found out what the noise was. The bar of soap Maryanne made fell off the edge of the sink. We must have knocked into the bathroom wall." My eyes investigated his as my face sagged with guilt. He came over to me, placing his hands on either side of my face before kissing my forehead.

"Hey, she'll be fine. From the things you've told me and what I've seen over the last two months, Maryanne's a strong girl. Everything's gonna be just fine."

As sweet as he was being, and as much as I hated to discredit what he was saying, my thoughts came flooding out along with a fresh bed of tears. "I just feel so bad for her. She thinks I abandoned her Mark! I just... I couldn't do it baby. I was getting so miserable. She stays home all day long with those kids, it's an awful life."

"It's not awful," he rebutted. "It's just not what you'd have picked for yourself. She isn't miserable, she just needs help. As much as we tried, ultimately her husband needs to be the one to help her out. Maryanne feels isolated, and as much as she loves your company, I know she wouldn't want you to feel isolated too."

"I really did want to help her." I sniffled before melting into his arms. "I know you did," he replied. "No more sad stuff, we moved away to lessen your stress. If you wanted to stay sad, we could have stayed," he joked. I swatted at his arm, wiped my eyes, and giggled,

"Nuh-nice Daddy." Something I often said to him when he teased me or when I got too callous with my own words.

We made it into town about two days later, ready to enjoy our true home, but utterly drained from the drive. I messaged Maryanne to let her know we arrived safely but got no response. Though it saddened me, I can't say I was surprised. I'd checked in periodically during the trip home with the same result. Maybe Mark was right, she just needed some time. If I still hadn't heard from her a week from now, I'd message Joey and ask him to put a word in for me.

Mark and I's work schedules caused us to miss each other for most of the first week home. There was next to no time to get settled in before they needed us back at our old jobs. Amidst the confusion, one of us had forgotten to turn the heat off. So, it should have been no surprise that we came home one day to a freezing cold camper. The propane tank sat sad and empty in its compartment. What was worse, an acrid stench assaulted my senses as soon as I stepped inside after a long day at work, like the smell of aspartame coating rotted meat. I couldn't help but gag as I opened the door and stepped inside. "Oh my god Mark!" I yelled. "What the hell is that?!?" I was annoyed that he not only hadn't heard me, but I turned around to find him not even in the house. He was standing outside on our makeshift patio area, his face scrunched into a look of deep confusion and concern. "Mark-"

He held a hand up to interrupt me. "So... I just got a message from Joey. Apparently, he hasn't heard from Maryanne all week either. The kids are freaking out and the guy's a fucking wreck." I felt the blood drain from my face, pooling at the bottom of my stomach before turning into an anvil of cold dread. "Do you have any idea where she could be?"

So many puzzle pieces clicked horrifically into place as I recalled the last two weeks of my life. Maryanne said so many things, made so many jokes that it was enough to concern me. I saw her in my mind, joking through the tears of heartbreak in her eyes. "Please don't leave me here. What if I just crawl into the trunk and come home with you?"

"Has he called the police?!?" His answer faded away under the booming voice of my worries, beyond intelligible. My eyes drifted to our bed. I hadn't done laundry for a good while, and we'd been wearing clothes out of our laundry sack to avoid moving things around too much. "M-Mark..." I stammered. "The bed," he didn't utter a word, didn't so much as grunt in acknowledgement. But I could tell by the look on his face that he was thinking the same thing that I was. He cautiously walked up the stairs, taking each one gingerly, like it might break beneath him as he stepped inside.

"No. It couldn't be. I don't mean to be an asshole here, but if she was in there, wouldn't there be some kind of I dunno... seepage?" He had a point, one that I took tremendous solace in. "Would you like me to check anyway? I highly doubt a thirty-four-year-old woman stowed away in the bed of our camper teenage prank style." I glared at him upon hearing those words, nodding my head firmly but with foreboding reluctance.

The smell intensified tenfold the moment he lifted our mattress. The clothes below were stained sickly shades of yellows and browns. That's why there was no liquid gathering on the floor, all of the fabric of our clothes and towels had absorbed it. I instructed him to lift higher, horrifically aware of what I would see underneath.

I recognized a wavy tuft of auburn hair sticking out from beneath a bundle of death-stained T-shirts. An involuntary scream of sorrow ripped through my lungs, causing Mark to accidentally drop the mattress. He backed away all the same, unwilling to investigate any further. I called the police to explain what had happened through torrents of tears as Mark called Joey. I could hardly hear his words through my own ripples of sobs, but I could tell by his tone that Maryanne's husband was inconsolable. Who the hell wouldn't be?!

The coroner explained that the only way Maryanne could fit herself inside was to wedge her spine at a crooked angle. The horrifying crack we had heard during our lovemaking was the sound of her neck breaking under our weight. We literally fucked on top of my dead best friend. The girl who had seen me through all of life's changes. The one I ran to in crisis and the first one to accept a twelve-year-old me into a new and frightening school.

We still are waiting to find out if we will be prosecuted. The only thing that saved us from immediate arrest was the chance that she had accidentally suffocated during the ride home. I say the word 'saved', but in reality, I think we deserve to go to jail for what we've done. I can't stop looking at the last line of the last poem she sent me, the last message I would ever receive from my best friend.

> *I just had to take time to tell you my dearest friend,*
>
> *in case you didn't know*

Anywhere that you call home, a piece of me will be with you when you go.

YOU ARE WHAT YOU MEAT

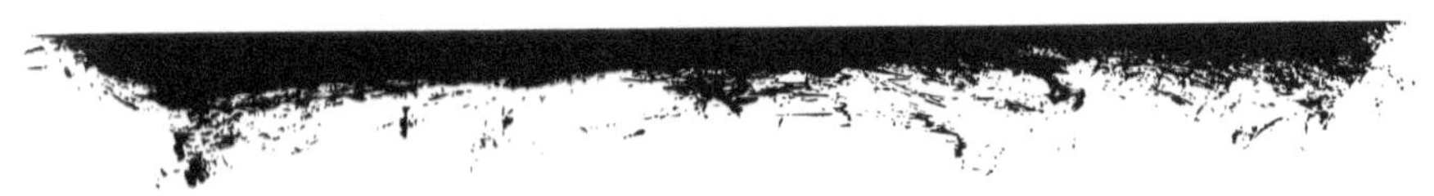

It was all I could do not to vomit when my mother—in-law proudly set the roast down in front of us, its meat glistening brown on the kitchen table. "Doug, are you alright?" My wife Maxine whispered, making sure her parents couldn't hear. She hadn't told them what I'd been through. Hell, I'd hardly had the mental strength to tell her everything myself. The smell of the freshly roasted meat created an acrid taste in the back of my mouth.

Ever since I was a kid, I'd been obsessed with experimentation. Scientific constants, variables, and results fascinated me. When other guys my age were mastering unhooking a bra with one hand, I was pouring salt on snails and making semipoisonous toxins with my chemistry set.

Before I had time to process, I'd signed an NDA, given over my bank account information to payroll, and had signed my first official contract in the scientific world as an intern. The feeling of knowing I would be welcomed into a community of peers that were into the same interests that I was. My mind raced at the possibilities of what my employer and I would discover together—the ways we would change the world as we knew it.

If only I'd have known...

When I walked in that first day, I was ready to take the world of science and medicine by the balls. The man who'd hired me would be the one I was working under. He told me nothing about himself other than that his name was Harris. Whether that was his first or last name, I had no idea. I didn't care much to ask at the time. Then again, I didn't think it was information that would be too relevant during an internship. People don't like an overabundance of questions, whether they'll admit it to you or not. And I didn't want to be the squeaky wheel that got boiled in hot grease.

Anyway, science is one of the broadest subjects that there is, and I knew I could have signed up to study any one of them. Being a student with military upbringing, I won't lie and tell you I wasn't hoping for something biochemical, or at the very least weather-related. Having said that, when Harris told me we'd be studying behavioral science, I was more than intrigued. The science of the mind hadn't even occurred to me as a possibility. With my family's various mental illnesses and addictions, I thought it'd be a wonderful area to study and understand. "Excuse me, Harris?" I said quietly. "Will we be studying serotonin levels and the effects of different chemicals on the brain?"

A thin smile stretched across his weathered face as he turned to acknowledge me. "That my good sir, is more psychological science. What we do here is different. You'd be hard pressed to find results like these in a Rorschach test or blood panel," he began to walk down a hallway to the left, wordlessly motioning for me to follow as he continued to speak. "You are here to learn, not to judge. Many aspiring scientists shy away from greatness... they let their moral compass get in the way. Is that going to be an issue Doug?"

I more than disliked the implications of his tone, but answered, nonetheless. "Of course, whatever you need sir-"

"HARRIS!" He barked, correcting a politeness that any other of my superiors would have appreciated. Harris then cleared his throat before addressing me in a softer voice. "Everyone here is perfectly aware of why they're here. They get compensation in the name of science. Now who wouldn't want that?" He smiled, resembling an old timey snake oil salesman. I merely nodded in response.

We entered a dark room that contained a long table and chairs. A pane of glass that took up the entire front wall, fully revealing the room behind it. Two women in nurses' scrubs sat in a bare, stark white room. There was nothing for them to sit on or lean against. It was just the two women, the floor, and a vast sea of maddening white. I stared at Harris, confused. "Don't worry, they can't see or hear us," he said matter of factly.

They looked bored and tired, but otherwise healthy. The complacency in their movements and facial expressions proved what Harris said earlier was true; these women were here of their own volition. We watched in silence for a full hour before Harris spoke again, shedding a very dim light on the point of the experiment. "These ladies here are vegetarian. Our job is to see how dedicated they are to their cause by testing their willpower and defenses. The first one to give into their hunger goes home with nothing. The woman who holds out the longest will receive a quarter of the money gathered for this research study, $10,800."

More silence continued, with even less activity coming from the inside. The taller woman with the dark hair seemed perfectly content with sitting idle and doing nothing. I'd surmised maybe she was a housewife or stay at home mom and desperately needed an empty space to herself (mostly). However, the shorter woman with the red hair became fidgety after only six hours. She began twisting her hair at the ends before ripping it off, chewing her fingernails and tapping her feet. I guessed that she was a smoker, someone who depended on an oral fixation.

I felt relieved at the end of the day when I got to go home. The plan was to go home and cook up the fattest, juiciest steak that I had in the freezer. I'd assumed that the women were released also, and were satiating their hunger with salads, veggies wraps or whatever the hell it was that they preferred to eat.

I was wrong.

The next afternoon, I was surprised to see the women in the same clothing they were in the day before. Their hair was disheveled, and dark bags were beginning to plague the skin under their eyes. "Jesus Christ, didn't they go home and eat?" I asked incredulously. My lower lip clamped under my top teeth the moment the inquiry came into the open, audible air.

Instead of snapping at me, I was surprised to see a smile form on Harris's normally joyless face. "I figured you'd ask. That's why I wanted you to be here when I fed them." My heart dropped as I saw him reach into a plastic container and pull out a raw hunk of fat-marbled beef, much like the one I'd selfishly grilled up and enjoyed the evening before. He sprinkled what looked like a mixture of pepper and rosemary before sliding it into the room on a tray. Both women looked at it disgustedly as it entered their shared space. I saw them murmuring things to each other but couldn't hear inside of the room.

"You can't be serious!" I exclaimed, much louder than I'd meant to. Harris shot me a steely look of warning as he withdrew the empty tray from the slot, closed the entrance to it and locked it.

I cringed as the taller woman dropped her pants and started urinating in the corner. Similar stains began to catch my eye the more I glanced around the room. The red-haired woman had reduced her nails to bloodied shards and still winced as she attempted to bite off more. Her swollen fingertips twisted off brittle bits of greasy hair. Harris grabbed a phone, clicked on a button, and leaned towards the opposite side of the room before whispering something I couldn't understand. As he did this, I realized that the red-haired woman wasn't trying to chew her nails at all. Instead, I'd noticed she was taking the ripped balls of hair and placing them between her teeth to chew on.

Two men walked into the white room with assertive steps. Everything inside of me screamed that I should have said something, anything, to try to stop what was going on in front of me.

But of course, I didn't. In my mind, it was all justified; they signed on for this. No one was forcing them to be here. The men grabbed the red—haired woman by the shoulders before forcing her to her knees. A single tear slid down her face as one of the men withdrew a pair of scissors from his inner coat pocket. The other produced what looked like a beard and moustache trimmer.

Within moments, the beautiful curls of red hair were nothing more than stolen wisps on the floor, dying more by the second. The women looked at each other as the clippers turned on, the blonde giving the other a nod of encouragement and solidarity. The room was swept and vacuumed before the pair left the same way that they'd come in.

You know what? This whole thing would be a hell of a lot easier if I just gave them names. I'd decided to call the taller, blonde woman Barbara and the other Rebecca. I wasn't privy to their real names, but it felt disrespectful to label them as Subjects A and B as Harris had in past statements.

The steak still sat between them, and I gagged to see some of the rust-red hairs from Rebecca's head stuck to its flesh. Oxidization had begun to set in at the corners, slowly turning the once crimson meat to a dull, rotted brown. I couldn't help wondering which one of them would crack first, or how long they'd have to stay if neither one did.

After two days off, I almost didn't go back. But Harris's words plagued me each time I thought about it, "Many aspiring scientists shy away from greatness... they let their moral compass get in the way. Is that going to be an issue, Doug?" So, after much mental rationalization and justification, I showed up bright and early Monday morning as promised. In my mind, I knew there was *no way* that the women would still be in there. Surely one of them pulled a Fear Factor and bit off a chunk of the meat by now.

But as per the theme of this story, of course, I was wrong.

Their once bright room had now become dingy under the pristine lights. Brown smears adorned the back of their clothes, excrement that had made it past the self-made defecation corner. As off point as it was, I remember wondering how one could shit so much with virtually nothing in their stomach. Barbara lay sleeping in the fetal position on the floor, surely weakened from the lack of nutrients and hydration. *Eleven thousand dollars had the potential to be a life-changing amount of money, but was it worth all this?* I thought sadly. Rebecca crawled weakly to the front of the room, sniffing the steak before dribbling bile down her chin. I gagged a little myself once I saw that the piece of meat was now tinged a sea algae green, with grey marbling swirled through it where the fat once was.

I bit my lip as she lifted the meat up to her face and couldn't help but breathe a sigh of relief as she tossed it away. Then I saw something that scared me. Rebecca looked at Barbara; a wild look had taken over her face. She was... studying her, eyeing her. I'd heard a lot of my friends rudely refer to girls as pieces of meat, but this was the first time I'd ever seen that saying personified on someone's face.

Now, what I said earlier about the NDA, I realize this entire thing is a direct defiance of that order. If legal ramifications fall upon me after this, I welcome them with open arms. The truth is, I'd be safer in jail, anyway.

What happened next shouldn't have been a surprise. This was a behavioral study after all, and people are capable of almost anything when pushed too far. Still.... I didn't see it coming; I don't think any of us did.

Rebecca made a coo-ing motion with her lips as she softly stroked Barbara's hair. The woman stirred slightly as Rebecca's shaved head leaned down to kiss her cheek. In a snap-like motion, she reared her head back and viciously buried it in the corner of Barbara's neck. Her eyes snapped open in surprise as Rebecca sent blood and sinew spewing from her own neck. Rebecca paused only slightly to write something on the floor in Barbara's blood. By the time anyone had gotten in there, it was too late. Rebecca knew to bite the most lethal part of the body, cutting off her air supply and blood flow instantly. She smiled through flesh covered teeth and she continued to eat her way up her right cheekbone.

———————

I snapped my attention back to my mother in law's kitchen table, shuddering away from the array of meats and vegetables piled high on plates. She'd been trying to speak with me, but I'd been too wrapped up in my own horrors to realize it. "Go on and eat Doug, while it's fresh!"

———————

I wasn't one of the men who busted in the room the women were being held. I ashamedly stayed behind... frozen in horror like a coward. But when I was questioned, they showed me a picture of what Rebecca had written on the floor. The words haunt me to this day, forever burned into my memory in an emblazoned red font.

IF YOU'RE GOING TO MAKE ME EAT MEAT, IT HAS TO BE FRESH.

I don't think I want to be a scientist anymore.

THE UNTETHERING

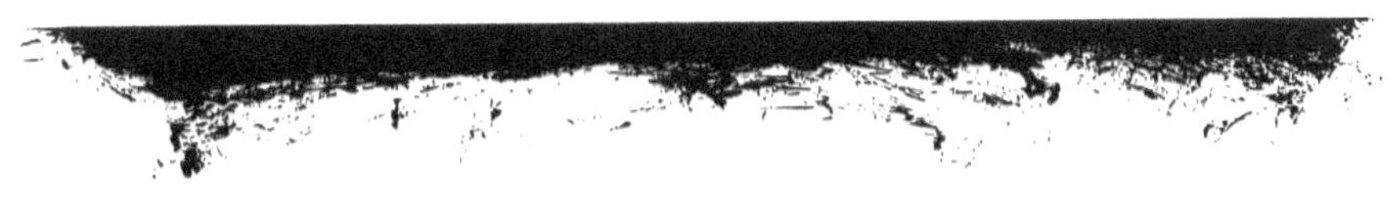

My boyfriend Justin, who for a long time was the love of my life, has turned into the object of my worst nightmare.

We met at a bowling alley when I was halfway through my teenage years. He had just entered his twenties. The age difference wasn't evident immediately; we were so taken with each other that we didn't think to ask. He called me every chance that he got after that first night.

I'd never been with anyone intimately and though we definitely had the chance, Justin never pushed me. He was sexually experienced, had a full-time job, and sold grass on the side to boot. We would get together anytime that we could during the weekends. I was a high school girl who still lived with mommy and daddy. I didn't even know how to smoke a cigarette without exhaling through my nose. While Justin had been shown pleasures and had real, adult experiences with *women*. Normally, the pressure of a situation like this would break lesser girls, but not me. Justin was happy just to be with me. We didn't have to smoke, fuck, or do anything other than hold each other, talk, and laugh. It was my first *pure* relationship. My heart broke to see it end. The best summertime romances usually do, though, right? The good ole' Danny and Sandy scenario.

Justin had come to my town with his friend Vance for a funeral. Vance's mother had killed herself. All these years later and I still don't know how or why… but that's for another day. Well, when it was time for Vance to go back home to a state that was practically across the country, Justin had no choice but to leave with him.

We both moved on with our lives, but the thought of Justin always sat dormant in the back of my mind, as first loves often do. I married young, built a home with my husband, and gave him two sons. Unbeknownst to me, he did just about the same. Both of our paths ended in divorce, and that's what started the pathway of bullshit and destruction that led us up to this point.

Hey! Remember me?

One message, just one social media message, started me on the path to Hell. Yeah, I know, I didn't have to respond, sure. But I wanted to. My heart and mind were entranced with the fact that he even remembered who I was and that I once meant something to him. It all felt so wonderful. We fell right back into the groove we found together fifteen years earlier.

It was only the natural order of things that we met up again. He drove all the way across the country nonstop to see me. We played house for a wonderful four days. I don't need to tell you the details, you already know we slept together. It was so much more than that, though. It was… talking and laughing and reeking of garlic from dinner together. He taught me new things and looked at me in a way I had never felt before. I thought that I had done the same for him. I'd desperately hoped, anyway.

As high as we rose together towards the heavens of soul-entwining bliss, we came crashing down to hell that much harder.

At first it was little things; I went from hearing every aspect about his day to entire twenty-four hour periods with no contact. I guess I shouldn't say no contact. I tried to get a hold of him plenty, to no avail. He would call me later; tell me he was depressed because of the distance and didn't feel like talking. Then we both got jobs with clashing schedules. Then a week went by. This excuse was that his mother was dying, and he was tending to family matters. Next thing I know I couldn't reach him for a month...I didn't know if he was dead, sad, fucking someone, etc. Eventually I gave up and we fell out of touch for over a year. He wrote to me to apologize one day out of the blue, just like the first time.

I forgave him, we once again picked up where we left off. The disappearances happened a few more times over the next year; but I'd always take him back. I know, I know... fool me once, shame on me. Fool me twice, shame on you. But I'd loved this man for half of my life.

I'd mostly kept all thoughts about Justin to myself. I hadn't had that many friends locally, and the ones I'd bare my soul to all lived out of state. What other option was there? I even went to therapy, for God's sake. It's not like I could afford to drive twenty-two hours cross-country or book a plane ticket just to ask why the fuck someone was ignoring me. I'm fairly sure they have shows on ID Discovery about that kind of behavior, anyway. Glenn Close flashed through my mind repeatedly in her white dress, "I will NOT be ignored!" That's not who I wanted to be.

I finally opened up to a close friend Wayne about all that I'd been going through after texting Justin that my father was in the hospital and him asking for cigarette money in response. This wasn't the man I'd known and loved since my heart was old enough to know how to feel the act. Whatever magic we did have was blackened and twisted into a symbiotic need on both parts. I needed my heart to catch up with reality. Anyway, my friend told me about this ritual, metaphorical healing more than anything else really.

"Natalie, I know this sounds weird, but the next time you take a shower, bring a pair of scissors into the tub with you. Scrub yourself as clean as you can and while you rinse off, cut the water droplets in the air. Speak your pain aloud about how they've made you feel. Shout the truths that your subconscious won't let your heart absorb. Make a cut with each declaration. Then when you're done, scrub your tub. Clean it as well as you possibly can; smudge it afterwards if you want to." Wayne said, clearing his throat before waiting for me to ask the questions I no doubt had formed.

My mind was having a hard time processing the information. "But... Justin doesn't give a shit if my tub's clean or not." I quipped.

Wayne chuckled in response. "I know right? That's what I said too initially. But try it. You have nothing to lose."

"What is it supposed to do? Like what's the purpose?" I inquired.

"Well, it's quite metaphorical really. It represents you cutting mental and emotional ties to the person intended. You're cutting the emotional tether, releasing yourself from the power they hold over you."

I agreed and disconnected the call. Wayne hadn't known it, but I was getting ready to take a shower just before he called. The scissors resting on the corner of the sink from trimming my hair the night before only solidified my resolve. It seemed like fate had given me everything I needed to be on my way to a better mindset. Fresh tear tracks cascaded down my cheeks, feeling like acid dripping slowly towards my breaking heart. I'd put my heart and soul into a relationship for two years, only to figure out that a lifetime wouldn't have been enough. My mind was consumed in a spider's web of questions, each branching off into three other questions of their own. Ultimately, I knew I could have asked all of them and the answers wouldn't matter. Nothing matters to someone who has given away their soul.

So, just as instructed, I followed the uhhh... exercise? I guess that would be the right word. I don't know. The important thing is that I did it. There were so many tears and cuts. It surprised me just how painful the words were to say. My bathroom tub was the cleanest it had ever been. The smell of bleach and burnt sage lingered on my skin and throughout the entire bathroom. I can't say I felt any different after. That wouldn't be put to the test until I heard from him again. Hopefully, the next time he dragged himself out of the shadows to grace me with his presence, I'd be ready.

Exhausted in every way possible, I laid down in bed. It barely took any time at all to surrender to the sweet, painless pull of sleep.

I spent the whole next week slowly clearing all signs of Justin from my life. I changed my phone number and blocked his email addresses. Not that this meant a damn thing until I blocked him from my Facebook, but there were some pictures I needed off of there that I wasn't ready to look at yet. Besides, it's not likely that he'd contact me anyway, right? This was more symbolic for me than anything else.

I slept in the next day, waking early the next afternoon, well past the time of singing birds and rooster crows. Justin was normally the first thing on my mind, and he definitely was that morning, but not in the same regard. His memory was wispy, almost ethereal. Like the memory of someone who had long since passed. And better yet, my bathroom was clean, although the scissors, which I had so delicately placed on the corner of the tub, were now gone. To avoid any future pain and drunken stalking, I opened up the Facebook app and went to Justin's page, fully intent on blocking him from my social media life.

My heart felt like it froze in mid-beat. The all-too—familiar tears that Justin assaulted my eyes flowed with different intentions now.

There were at least a dozen posts on his wall, including a one from his mother in bold print. She posted a message that Justin was found dead in his apartment that morning. The cause of death wasn't apparent at first. I had to message the few friends that he had that knew of my existence to find out what exactly happened. His....*wife* (ouch) had come home after staying the night at a family member's house to find him in their bedroom, dead.

This was the part that made my blood run cold. Guys, I'm not a violent or vindictive person. I've never wanted to hurt anyone, let alone kill them. I did what I thought I had to do in order to save myself, but I never would have done anything if I thought it had any literal consequences. I cut air and water, that's it! Anyway, the thing that terrifies me, the thing that directly lets me know it's my fault, is that Justin had died from multiple stab wounds. Most were shallow, but the deepest and fatal blow was evident by the wound in his heart.

The exercise was supposed to cut our ties forever, but now Justin will haunt me for the rest of my life. I know this, because I can see him standing by my window when the lightning flashes on stormy nights. There was a time where I'd have given anything for him to be within 100 feet of me, now I can't get far enough away.

UNWANTED VISIONS OF THE FUTURE

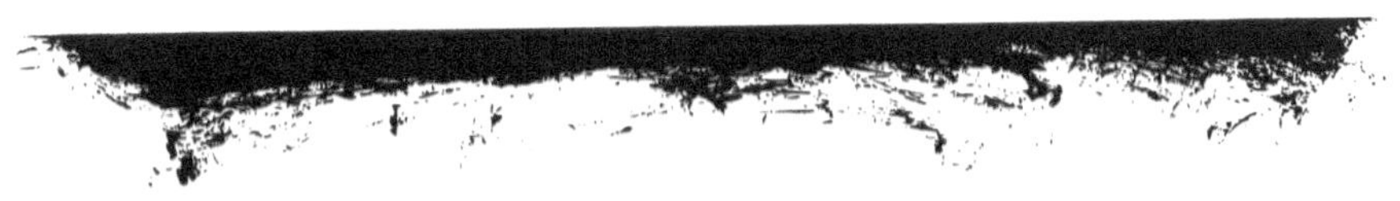

It wasn't any day out of the ordinary, towards the end of summertime. All the kids were about to go back to school. At first, people thought the televisions were a prank. Just some teenagers getting the last of the craziness out of their system before buckling down for another year of school. Most of the people in our small town in Virginia assumed they were broken. They took them out to the side of the road to be picked up with the rest of the trash.

My wife Ana and I had just moved here about two months ago. I was offered an amazing job opportunity that couldn't be passed up.

We wanted a better life for our children and, as hard as it was to leave our families behind, we made the move. Things were great at first glance. We loved the new school that the kids were zoned for. People in town waved at one another. It was like something out of an old TV show.

Virginia weather is nothing at all like Georgia's is. That's where we had come from. It's nice to be able to go outside more and enjoy nature without being cooked alive.

There were barbecues, fireworks, tire swings at the lake... I couldn't imagine much mischief could take place in a town like this. But I was wrong. That's what happens when you make assumptions, especially about a whole town of people.

Something isn't right here, not by a long shot. However, we had sacrificed everything that we had in order to move here. There's no other option but to stay and make this opportunity work; for better or for worse.

Anyway, back to the TVs. They were old, assorted models. Most of the ones that we had as kids; before the flat screen came out.

They don't offer any high definition. You can't connect them to the internet. If you were lucky enough, you'd be able to get one with a VHS player attached on the bottom.

That's not the case now, though. My mind reels about thinking of the models left on doorsteps with VHS attachments.

Are there tapes in them? Have the people even checked? I don't know whether to feel sorry for them or thankful that I wasn't one of them; although this scenario's left me thinking that there isn't much to be thankful for, not... not anymore.

See, people think they want the answers to life. The ultimate question, the only one that really matters when it comes down to it, is death.

How am I going to die? How old will I be? Will I be alone? Will my children go before me?

I used to be one of those people, but now I have my answer. And will spend every second left of my living life wishing I never got it.

There weren't any knocks on the door. The doorbell didn't ring. I just simply woke up, opened my front door to smoke a cigarette and there it was; an old Magnavox television set.

It wasn't dusty. It looked like it was in good condition. The screen even still shined. But this didn't belong to me. It couldn't have. I threw out this exact same television set over twenty years ago.

I had seen an uprising in an older television set being set out on the curb. I didn't do this with that one. Nostalgia caused me to bring it right inside to see if it still worked. Something inside of me shifted the instant the screen clicked on. First, there was only static, along with indecipherable white noise. But soon, the reflection that stared back at me through the television screen changed.

I was older… but not elderly. Hints of gray had just started to flirt with the hair on my temples. Silver streaks shone through the red of my beard. I'll have to admit, for a second, vanity took hold before rationality. A little older? Yes. A little gray? Absolutely. But I still looked damn good.

The surroundings in the television screen warped and changed. The scene depicted a dark and dingy hospital room. I am laid up in bed; an oxygen mask was placed over my face, and it looked like I was being fed intravenously.

A dark figure crept ever closer to me from a far corner. His body was monstrously thin and rigid. Bones protruded from his back like he was preparing to shift forms. Where his face should have been there was only a static filled screen. I'm not being colorful either. He literally had a television screen for a face. Images of my contorted and twisted body suddenly flipped through it. This thing was channel surfing through every level of pain the human body could experience.

My body was riddled with tubes, the largest one inserted at the base of my throat. It was like watching a movie; all fuzziness and static had left. Leaving a terrifying clarity to the screen. I ridiculously called out to myself; screamed at myself to turn around. I half expected the other me to hear. He… well… I should say, I did not hear.

My wife sat in a small chair next to the shell of my body. Her slender frame wracked with stifled sobs. While still beautiful, stress and sorrow hadn't been as kind to her aging process as it had been to mine. Before the cancer, that is. She looked withered; her eyes held no hope.

A doctor came into the room and told her that they had done all they could treatment wise. But unfortunately, it had spread too far to be helped. They said those fatal words, giving my murderer a name, advanced stage esophageal cancer.

My thumb flew to the power button and pressed it. I didn't want to see any more, know anymore, or hear anymore. If I turned it off before seeing anything more, I could still chalk it up to insanity. This wasn't real.

But the television wouldn't turn off. I reached for the cord, ready to yank it out of its outlet and take the whole thing to the trash. The moment my fingers wrapped around it; my wife asked a question.

"If we had caught this sooner, would you have been able to save him?"

The doctor looked at her and shook his head, telling her that at this point it was hard to say. It was a miracle that I had survived this long with this much damage to my throat. She then asked how long ago he thought the cancer had developed and said that I'd been having problems with my voice. She said I'd been losing it off and on for the past four years or so. She explained how I worked at a job where I had to yell all the time. We figured that's what the strain on my voice was from.

The doctor replied that sometimes... in such cases, it can be treated and go into remission. However, in my case, losing my voice was likely signs of the cancer gaining strength, expanding. Even if we had found it two years ago, there wouldn't have been much different of an outcome.

I yanked the cord out of the wall with all of my might, trying to end my misery. The screen shut off, white flashing through black. In those final moments, just as the white flashed before the screen was consumed with black, I saw so many flashes of many things.

Once you see the static man, you'll always be on his radar. He will start to make himself known in your real world. And the closer he gets to you, the closer your death follows behind.

So please... I am begging you. If you wake up one morning and find a television on your porch, get rid of it! Do not bring it into your home. Do not plug it in because if you do... you'll find out all the things that you don't want to know. I did... I've seen how I die, and I've seen how you all do too.

Believe me, it's not something you want to know.

GHOST WHALE

"Be respectful to the ocean and its creatures, and it will be respectful to you."

My mother said this to me throughout my entire life growing up in Japan, her and my Dad loved to fish. I never understood what she meant. How could I be respectful to the ocean while ensnaring and killing the fish that lived within it?

I asked her this one day, and she pointed to a boat approaching the open water. It was tan and brown with a siren attached to the front.

"That right there darlin' is the department of Fish and Wildlife. Believe me, you don't wanna get in trouble with those people. There's almost nothing scarier; not even the actual Police."

My young mind had a hard time grasping such a concept.

"Well... then why are they here now?"

"They're here because somebody did something to upset the natural balance of the ocean. There are certain laws that people on land must abide by to keep the ocean as beautiful as it is for future generations.

For instance, take the red fish. They have a lot of them in the United States where I grew up before we moved here. Legally, you're only allowed to keep a redfish if it's between a certain length. Anything over or under that has to be thrown back. There are other kinds of fish that you're only allowed to catch one or two of because their species is so limited in numbers."

This answer didn't quite satisfy me.

"Mama you said almost there's almost nothing scarier. What happens to the ocean when Fish and Wildlife aren't there to protect it?"

"Ahhh... That my dear, is where the Bake—kujira comes in. The Bake-kujira is one of the largest whales in God's creation. It's a spirit of the water; a guardian almost. If you're unfortunate enough to see him, you know you did something really bad. The Bake-kujira only shows up in severely mistreated waters; granting tragedy and misfortune to all that are around to see it.

"Its skin is dark as death and its bones show through patches in its ethereal body. It summons great storms. Boats shatter and splinter apart; the waves slicing through them like razors. Winds whip the water into a vortex of death, subjecting all who are near to the possibility of a watery grave."

The area that we live in is eighty percent surrounded by water. Mother told me she taught about this creature to potentially save my life one day. She died when I was seventeen.

It seems like a lifetime has passed since then. Now I'm grown with a husband of my own. We've been together for four years and are expecting our first child in six short months.

My husband works on a fishing charter, along with most of the men that grew up here. It's not uncommon for him to be gone for weeks at a time with little to no contact.

I never told him about the Bake-kujira, believing it to be a silly fisherman's urban legend. The tale stayed with me, though. It flashed through my mind every time he told me he'd be going out on a job.

His latest trip was especially long, to the point where I was out of my mind with worry. Sleepless nights plagued my existence. Every potential sound of him coming through the door was met with disappointment.

When he finally did come home, he stunk of mold and rot. There was an insanity in his eyes that I hadn't seen before. His face was pale as paper and gaunt.

"Ken, what happened?!? You look like you've seen a ghost." I ran to his side, my voice growing louder with every syllable.

He told me through drunken breaths that in a way, he had. He said that they were almost ready to come in when he spotted something about a hundred yards out in the sea. It looked like it was swimming right for their boat. The closer it got, the more violent the water became. The ripples invite the boat to a dance of its own destruction. It was the largest creature he had ever seen. It was the size of ten whales, he said, although I find that hard to believe since they were in partial darkness.

His voice starts to tremble as he tells me it had no eyes and was showing no signs of changing its trajectory with the boat. No matter how much they increased speed, they wouldn't have been able to reach the shore before it reached them.

I selfishly interrupt him; knowing full well he won't understand my question.

"Well, were you mistreating the fish? Did you catch everything you caught or abide by fishing laws?"

He gave me an incredulous look through bloodshot eyes.

"No. Of course not. We always do things legally when it comes to what we catch. Do you think I want F&W on my ass?!?

Anyway, we all braced ourselves to prepare for this thing's impact. But nothing happened. After a moment or two of waiting longer than necessary, I ran to the edge of the boat and looked out over the water.

This thing's tail was swimming right through the boat. It was... it was like it was invisible. Just passed through the boat, like poof! The way you see the ghosts on TV walk through walls. I can't understand it. After that, the water got really rough. Thankfully, we were close enough to the shoreline to make it on land before the storm hit. Except... after we docked, no storm came. The weather was perfectly calm and unremarkable."

I welcomed him into our bed with open arms that night. He falls asleep with his head against my swollen stomach. No matter how I try, I can't get his story out of my mind, and how much it reminds me of what my mother had told me.

A bang on the door wakes us from a blissful sleep. Someone's knocking far too aggressively than necessary for this time of morning.

Two men in suits with badges were on our front porch, holding a warrant for my husband. He was arrested and charged with homicidal kidnapping and murder.

My mother had warned me about disturbing the peace of the ocean through respecting fishing laws. She said nothing however, about how the bake-kujira felt about dumping bodies into it.

I guess my husband found that out the hard way.

HAVE YOU MADE YOUR CONTRIBUTION?

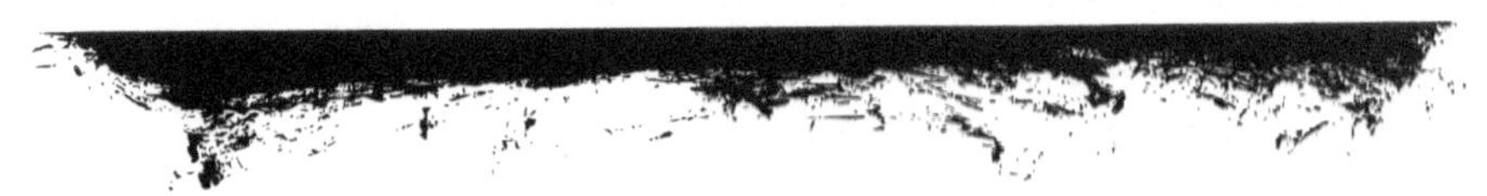

A familiar woman runs towards me. A small child sits perched on each hip, jostling with every one of her fervent steps. One is crying from having just been preemptively unlatched from her still hanging breast.

"Della? Oh, my goddess, HELLO!"

She wraps me up in a protective hug. Each child's face squishes awkwardly against both sides of my own breasts.

"Hello!"

I respond confidently. I wonder how long we are going to play the small talk game before she realizes I don't remember her whatsoever; let alone her name.

"How have you been? Goodness, it's been so long! It's been what...? How many years now?"

I ask her, hoping her answer will lead to some kind of recognition.

"Easily since tenth grade. Your cousin came to the compound just before we moved. My family left after... well, that's not important. All that matters is that I'm here now."

"The month I turned eighteen, I walked out of my front door, drove out here and never looked back."

Jesus, I think to myself. Why the fuck would anyone who actually got to escape ever want to come back? My family has been stuck here our whole lives. They don't acknowledge any other way of life.

A pert clearing of her throat breaks me from my inner monologue.

"What about you? How have you been doing? Your hair has gotten so long! You've always been such a pretty lil thing. Have you made your contribution? Murph and I have six now! Can you believe it?"

She inquires, eyes alight with the anticipation of my response. I knew this was coming, I'm just surprised it took her so long.

"Yep! I have a daughter, Sasha. She's seven years old. It took us a little while at first, but she was worth every heartbreak along the way."

The smile I've practiced to the point of obsession peels across my lips. It's extremely important to crinkle the corners of my eyes to make it look real. No one's gonna believe me if I'm dead faced.

"Just one then? Are you planning for another?" The woman asks warily. I still don't know her goddamn name!

Well, this was certainly new. Usually telling these people I have a child, a daughter no less, satiates them enough to stop their questions.

The smile fades from my face one muscle at a time in preparation for the next part of my answer.

"Erm... no; not yet, anyway. We lost Sasha's father when she was five. I haven't gathered the courage to try again."

Her face puckers like she just performed fellatio on a lemon.

"Oh, goodness, I'm so sorry! I had no idea! Me and my big mouth, right? Listen, I've been married a long time, but you can always talk to me alright? Give me your phone so I can give you my number."

Finally, I'll know her damn name!

"Of course! Thank you so much, I'd like that."

She types in her contact information and hands it back. Maya... her name is Maya.

One more smile makes an appearance on my face as I turn to leave the encounter. My feet almost make it out of the aisle when I hear her call after me.

"Ya know it's never too late, right? Children are our future. You never know what contribution your children will make to our World."

That conversation pretty much tells you a lot of what you need to know about the community that we live in.

A flyer for the town meeting is perched under my windshield wiper. I remove it with more than a little annoyance and get in the car. The drive home depresses me. I've driven it dozens, if not hundreds of times. I know where all the holes in the fence are. Sasha and I always sing a silly song during those parts to distract her; but I look. Years of conditioning and cognitive mental therapy scream at me not to look, but I do every time just the same.

Passing glances provide me with different views of horror. The women are dirty; literally dressed in rags. Their faces are haunted with years of neglect. To our town they are refuse, a waste of the human populace.

Being childless robbed them of the blessings and way of life the contributors experienced. 'The Barren', as they call them, are forced to contribute in other ways. These women are farmhands, overworked cooks (not even allowed to eat the food they make), landfill workers, medicinal experimentees and so forth.

I am supposed to be one of them.

My mind takes me back to a place in time just before Sasha became mine.

A distant wailing woke Sharon and I from a deep sleep one evening. Our limbs lingered in their embrace longer than necessary for the situation, hoping it was the remnants of a dream.

Sharon was the first one dressed. She ushered me over to our bedroom window to peer outside. I ran over to her, almost forgetting to leave the socially acceptable amount of space between our anxious bodies.

The street looked quiet, empty even. No one was outside. Everything was still, save for the shivering of the leaves from the cold night air. Only one car was on the street. The lights inside were on; the silhouette of the person inside was completely immobile. It was definitely apparent that they weren't the ones making the noise.

Although Sharon challenged me, I was the one who went outside to investigate. Someone out there needed help, I was sure of it.

Each step towards the car felt like it slowed a consecutive second in time. The last steps seemed to take hours. My hand froze mere inches before knocking on the glass. The scene seized any communication between my brain and body. I found myself temporarily frozen in place; my sanity not allowing me to move until I could make sense of what I was seeing.

A dark-haired woman sat in the driver's seat. She didn't look to be much younger than myself at the time. Her once brown eyes were cloudy and lifeless; frozen in an eternal thousand-yard stare. There's foam crystalized at the corners of her lips. A needle hangs limp in her arm, still embedded in a vein.

The worst part of all this was what was in the back seat.

A red-faced baby girl, not more than three or four months old, cried incessantly in her car seat. Her voice was strained from calling out. Her eyes were just barely to the point of producing tears.

I unbuckled her and rocked her in my arms, making sure to survey the street for onlookers or gapped curtains. Thankfully, there were none.

Sharon gently took the baby from me and held her to her chest. In a split-second moment of doubt, I ran out and unbuckled the car seat to take inside with me.

Looking back now, it's a miracle we held it together through it all. Timing was heavily in our favor. Whether it was God or Goddess, someone was definitely on our side that year. I've always been a bigger gal; it wasn't too much of a stretch to assume I was pregnant and didn't show. A close friend in need of a home agreed to act as her father in exchange for a place to live.

I wasn't lying earlier when I said we lost him when Sasha was five. Not everyone can make it here. The way people are raised makes them genuinely believe they can't have a successful life anywhere else. Mitch ate a bullet one night after dinner, and that was that.

I kept to myself mostly. No one could know too much if they didn't get too close.

And, if you hadn't guessed by now... Sharon is not my cousin. Love doesn't mean much to a community that only cares about repopulation. If anyone knew what we really were, we'd be taken to the municipal office cells and offered what they call 'a choice.'

Those who are found to be living against 'their way of life' are brought into rooms full of voracious male occupants. Their pants clinging tightly to the growing bulges of their groins as they stare hungrily at whichever woman is brought in; like a raw steak tossed to a pit of starving hounds.

Town leaders arrive and offer two options to our kind. Women could consent to repeated sexual encounters with each of the men. Or choose not to and be tossed outside the walls of the comfortable compound with the other wastes of society. Those who chose the first option were housed and subjected to constant 'breeding rituals' until they became pregnant. If conception fails after one full calendar year, then they also get exiled outside of the compound walls for being a non-contributing member.

Rules were set into place to protect the physical safety of the women forced to live outside the confines of our walls, but they aren't usually enforced. More men travel outside of our walls each day to pillage and violate those poor women. Each being allowed discreet entry back after their varied conquests.

Women are beaten, sometimes to the point of death, and are provided no medical care. If someone gets sick, they're weeded out to make room for those more physically able to perform their tasks.

It isn't right, but who would stop them? The leaders that would hear their cries for justice are the very ones that put them there in the first place.

Flyers about town meetings were all over. It seems like every telephone pole, store bulletin boards, and town mailboxes were inundated with them. Everyone seemed swept up in it; even Sharon talked about going once or twice. Maybe it would look better if we went to blend in rather than stay away completely. At any rate, it doesn't matter now. Now I just want to love my girls.

Sasha's curls bounce playfully as she runs out to greet me. Even though she'll be taller than me soon, I still see that little red-faced baby... screaming in the face of death in that car.

"How's it going, baby girl? Did you have a good day today? I missed you!" I ask as I throw my arms around her, grocery bags hanging off wrists and all. She sees me struggling and takes the lighter bags so I can distribute the weight of the heavier ones more evenly. She's always been so sweet. It must have come from her biological family.

I was a terribly hateful child. It was made very apparent to me at an early age that I would have to fight for my right to be happy and safe in the World I grew up in. It resulted in a very guarded and lonely upbringing.

My daughter looks at me with sudden concern. "Mama Sharon isn't doing so well today. She's been doing that thing where she doesn't hear me and just stares out of the window. It creeps me out when she does that."

I try my best to force a giggle to pass it off as quirkiness or the effects of her mother being a deep thinker. In all reality though, I know what's coming.

Every once in a great while, my love gets down, really down. Like so down she can look up at a clear sky for hours and still not see the sun. It kills me to see the gorgeous blue eyes I fell in love with turn grey. It kills her that she can't be open about who she is... who we are. She hates it that she has to act like an extended family member to Sasha instead of her mother. So many times, in public, we've wanted to kiss, stare longingly... even a small brush of hands would mean so much sometimes. We can't do that, though.

Not to mention she's under pressure for not adding a contribution of her own. She's filed appeal after appeal, but her time had come due. She has four months left to become pregnant. But she refuses to share her body with anyone but me, no matter what the cost.

It has been affecting our sleep as well. I'd feel her fitful tossing and turning against me as we slept. Some nights I'll roll over and she wouldn't even be there at all. For the sake of the stress of that damned meeting in the early morning, I selfishly hope tonight isn't one of those nights.

Two melatonin gummies have me feeling relaxed and ready to fall asleep in a little over twenty minutes. My hunny was on her own tonight. This bitch (me) needs some much-deserved sleep.

Terrible dreams chase me all through my sleep. Suffocating plumes of smoke surround the room that I'm in. It's remarkably familiar but yet, not immediately recognizable at the same time. Men are clutching at their throats blindly. Some have blood and gore running down their face from gouged eyes, others have deep black, red stains spreading on the groins of their pants. Flames licked at the air from behind a closed door. No one could escape, and the fire wouldn't be held back for long.

My body jolts awake with a start; the taste of screams and ash still flavors my tongue. I cry out to Sharon through horrified tears, only to find that she isn't next to me. The sun's just starting to flirt with the tops of the trees, daybreak has just barely threatened to arrive.

The air feels... off. Our home is a little too peaceful, everything's unsettlingly still. The acoustics of the floorboards let me know that I'm about to enter a room with a heavy object in the middle of the floor.

"Sharon? It's me sweetheart. Are you alright, babe? I had a soul-fucking nightmare, and I need cuddles, okay?" My feet stop dead in their tracks. My body movements in response to the sight before me instantly take me back to finding Sasha as a baby.

Sharon is okay. She is alive, she is smiling. But she... well... she's definitely not the same. The love of my life sits in a disheveled clump on our living room floor. Her forearms and face are covered in blood, gore, and soot. Two orbs with brown irises are clenched tightly in her left hand. Her blue eyes stare up at me, beaming with pride.

"Dells my dearest, it's all gonna be okay. I got those evil bastards, and no one will ever have to hide who they are again. I've finally made my contribution."

TARYN

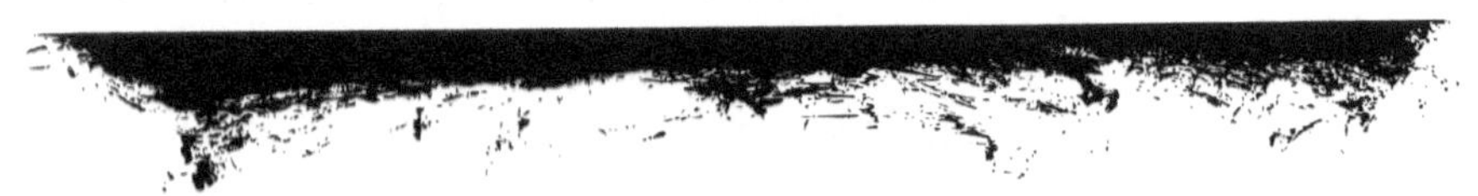

I replay it over and over again in my mind. We go out in the yard. I sit down. Taryn goes off to play with the neighbor boy, Clayton. I yell to her to be careful and stay away from the neighbor's old car.

Clayton falls and hurts his knee. Taryn is still in sight. I run to Clayton and lift him to see if he can put weight on his leg. As I help him stand; I look around the yard. Taryn isn't there.

We frantically search the house and call for her, no answer. I take Clayton home and ask his parents if they've seen Taryn. My wife stays by behind to call the police. After hours of searching the block, there's no sign of our little girl.

The first night without Taryn is torture. Her toys look so dark and sinister without her here to play with them. Stuffed animals aren't smiling. Doll's eyes aren't twinkling. The night crickets keep their voices to themselves.

We wake up early the next day, not that we got much sleep. Melodi and I search the neighborhood homes again. As heartbreaking as it is to do, we also search up and down the ditches on the sides of the road.

The rain's stopped, and it's getting hot outside. We follow neighborly interviews and call the police every morning. We gave out countless copies of our telephone number and called all of Taryn's friends' parents as well.

No one's seen our baby girl. At four years old, she wasn't likely to go extremely far by herself. The possibility that she'd been taken starts to become overwhelming. The heat beats down on us as we search through the woods. We look up and down streets and trudge through ditches. No Taryn, no hope, no love.

My wife and I aren't taking it very well. She grows more distant and poisoned with resentment by the minute. The fire of love in her eyes has frozen over like a winter tundra.

I lay awake at night, just staring out of the window. Sometimes I can swear I hear her underneath the sound of the wind through the trees. The dark night greets me with silence and a sickening feeling of dread. Thinking she's out there somewhere, all alone and scared.

Things finally came to a head on the fifth day Taryn's gone. Melodi starts in on me after hitting the bottle.

"Why weren't you paying attention to her? What were you doing? On the phone talking to your stupid friends? She was 5 feet away from you! How could you have let her disappear?! You've got to be one of the most thoughtless people I've encountered. You deserved for this to happen! But not our little girl... my little girl."

My wife won't stop. Her words become more lethal with every syllable she spits out. I'm ashamed to say that I'm past the point of mental restraint. My hand is larger than her face. I imagine crushing it like a cantaloupe.

I know exactly what will happen. I know she'll try to hit me, and I know that she will miss. I know that if I move my foot just 3 inches to the right, she will trip. I know when she trips, she will fall. And I knew that when she fell, her head would meet the corner of the glass countertop. Call it an accident of nature; and that's that.

I called the police and told them what happened. I step outside to smoke as many cigarettes as I can before they come to question me and take her body away.

It's windy outside today. I'm slapped in the face with something the second I step out the door. It's an awkward, sweet scent;

something not common to nature. I follow the direction of where it's coming from with my eyes.

My heart drops. I scream louder with every footfall closer to the neighbor's car. Child-proof locks… it has child-proof locks; the front doors are stuck. It was raining that day. I had yelled at her to stop playing around the car. We hadn't checked the car.

I look through the window; I already know what I'll see. If I squint my eyes shut really hard; when I open them again, for about the first seven seconds it looks like she's just taking a nap. But the discoloration of her skin returns along with my vision, and there's nothing I can do to ignore the smell.

THE SIGN OF A GOOD MOTHER

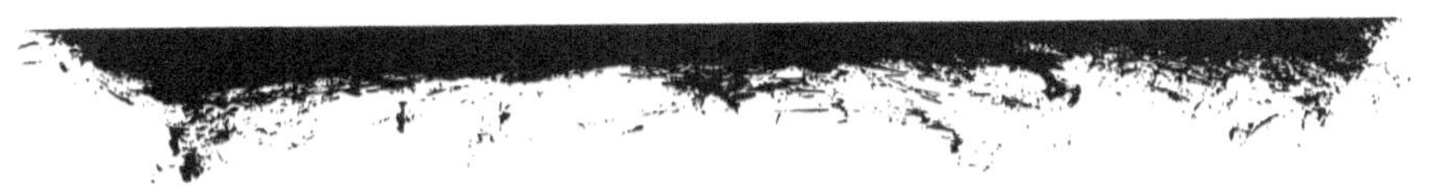

My eyes snap open as I'm forced awake by a sharp throng throughout my hip bone. Misty eyed from the pain, I have no choice but to roll over and try to stand. I rise with shaky legs and wait for the impending agony. One step down, twenty-five more to go till I'm in the bathroom. The second step takes place without much event, and then it hits.

Instantly I double over as I feel the sharp mass of pain drop deep into my pelvis. Ashamedly, I then recognized the sound of my bladder's failure sprinkle on the floor. There they are. At least I've made it to the third step this time, though! Usually, they hit me on the first or second. It's so helpful to have my feet fully on the ground beforehand to help absorb the pain a little.

I've looked forward to pregnancy for all of my adult life. I finally made it, thirty-two years old, thirty-nine weeks and four days pregnant with twin boys. We're naming them Christopher and William. My excitement over seeing our boys is almost palpable. Then, of course, there's the pain and discomfort. I can't wait for it to be over. Now I know I'm not the only woman in the world to have gone through this. However, I think it's borderline inhumane to make me go over thirty-eight weeks without so much as a mention of an induction.

The last two trimesters of my pregnancy were incredibly stressful. I had started bleeding heavily at eleven weeks. Fearing the worst, my husband Corey rushed us to the hospital, but they found absolutely nothing wrong. There were no internal abnormalities, and both babies looked perfectly fine. Aside from that, except for the constant gut-wrenching nausea, the last two-thirds of this pregnancy have passed without incident. The discomfort started at about thirty-two weeks but hadn't become unbearable until I hit thirty-seven. Now it was just sit and play the waiting game time.

I decided to try some of the wives' tale methods of naturally helping things along. There was lots of sex; doctor's orders! I did my best to stay more relaxed than usual. Corey may or may not have caught me eating raw pineapple with a hot sauce drizzle more than once. Nothing was working, and I was getting more miserable by the day.

The time came for my mom's daily phone call update. "Hey Mom. No labor yet. Yeah, I'm okay. Yes, the boys are fine. How are you and Dad?" I ask casually. "We're fine babe. Listen! What you need to do is have Corey go and drive you down a bumpy dirt road. That will speed things right along. Your grandmother took me down a bumpy road when I was pregnant with you and out you came the next day."

My mother has told me this a lot of times, but I never really considered taking her seriously until now. "Mom, how is that safe? That sounds like an aggressive way to start labo—"

Mom interrupted me. "You girls today. You get pregnant for the first time, and you think you know better than everyone. Why do you think they tell you to have sex? What do you think that is? It's jostling, your womb needs to be jostled. And what a ride!" She laughed loudly and dirtily. "Mom...... I can't even. Gross. Everything is fine. I promise when it's time, you'll be the first to know, okay. I love you."

I hung up and told Corey what my mother had told me. He shakes his head with a smile. "Sure! Okay, let's just shake the baby out. Isn't there a syndrome for that? Yeah. that's how bad it sounds to me."

One of the baby's kicks hits my cervix and I cry out, making hot tears prick the corners of my eyes. He rushes up to hold my hand just as I reach out for his arm to lean on. "Baby, I really don't see what it would hurt to try. I can't do this anymore. You can't go to your doctor and demand an induction without a valid medical reason. They're so cramped in there. They'll probably grow up claustrophobic from this, you know?" I say to him, half joking and half pleading.

So, we leave to head off into the woodsy part of town. All the best dirt roads were out here. Corey stops at the beginning of the first one that we came across. "Are you sure you want to do this? You know I'll always support whatever you decide." I nod, double check my seat belt and put my hand on the dashboard to somewhat brace myself.

The first couple of roads were uneventful. The most that happened was I may have peed a little. By now it was dark outside, the only visibility coming from the headlights of our car. We turn down a road that's slightly wider than the ones we drove over before. I wasn't enjoying this at all.

I had momentarily taken off my seat belt to try to ease a cramp out of my ribs when we hit. Due to the absence of streetlights, we don't see the huge hole to the left of our path. My body bounces violently, slamming my side against my passenger door. A burn radiates throughout my torso that makes me scream out in pain, accompanied by a great gush of fluid. I look down to see red spreading throughout the middle of my jeans and the seat of the car.

"Corey! Take me to the hospital. Something is wrong." I command through tears. The horrifying red of my fingertips glistens in the moonlight. They hook me up to the fetal monitors. The nurse reading the screen tries to hide the falling of her face, but I see it.

She rushes out of the room and comes back in with a doctor dressed in mint green scrubs. "Mrs. Davitt, we are having trouble finding the second baby's heartbeat. Now there can be a lot of reasons for this that are perfectly harmless. Just to be safe though, we are gonna go ahead and bring those little guys out into the world today. We're going to perform a cesarean section delivery to speed things up a bit. Sound good?" He gives me a thin smile, eyebrows raised with the anticipation of confirmation.

I'm in so much pain at this point, all I can do is look at my husband. He nods and gives me the most encouraging smile that he can manage. My voice is little and raspy, almost foreign to my ears. "Whatever you think is best to do. I just want them to be okay. The pain... something's wrong. Please." My eyelids become heavy and although I know I should be panicking, I feel strangely at peace.

I wake up in a light blue recovery room. There is a bouquet of daisies on my bedside table beside a pitcher of water. Corey is there, his eyes swollen and red rimmed from crying. In his arms, I see a neatly packed bundle of blue blanket; a blue cap sticking out of the top. He starts walking over to me and places a baby in my arms. "Are you sure you're awake enough to hold him?" He asks me warily. After I nod that I am, he continues. "Honey, I'm so sorry. I'll never forgive myself. One of our boys, our smaller one, didn't make it. He got knocked loose from your placenta and by the time we got to the hospital, it had been too long."

I sit there almost numb. My eyes haven't even managed to look at who I'm holding yet. The only thing that I can sputter out is, "Wh... which one did we agree the smaller baby was? William or Christopher? I need to know for when we have a service for him." His face grimaced before bursting out in fresh tears. "Oh baby, I'm so sorry. William is the one we lost. You're holding Christopher," he gives a heaving nod towards the sleeping bundle in my arms.

Finally, I manage to look down. He is absolutely perfect. "Well look at you! Hi there." I coo. He wakes up upon hearing me speak to him. There he is, our Christopher. A strawberry blond curled cherub with the biggest dark blue eyes. "I'm gonna love you extra hard. You probably miss your brother, huh, baby?" It was at this point that my emotional dam shattered. The tears start coming and it doesn't feel like they would ever stop. "You don't have to be sad, Christopher. William will always be with you." I say to him, trying to sound as soothing as I can.

It's two weeks after the service; we are home and settled. I have started to crawl out from under my rock of despair inch by inch. Corey came home a day before we did. He wanted to make sure everything was as easy as possible for me, separating the pairs of baby items from two to one. The name William was scraped off of the wall and painted over to match the rest of the room. Not that I wouldn't always see the letters through the paint, even if no one else did.

I haven't spoken to my mother since giving birth. She of course attended the service. My brothers and Corey did a good job of providing a subtle barrier between her and myself. It wasn't her fault, not directly, but I can't help my dark thinking. If I hadn't followed her advice, I would be somewhere else at that moment, struggling with two newborns and not in a funeral parlor with just one. The casket is so small that it doesn't even seem like it should ever have been made. Death of human beings that tiny have no place in nature, but they get sold every d ay.

My mother wants to come by the house today-two weeks later—to check on Christopher and me. The selfish part of me wants to say I'm looking forward to her visit just to save face. However, that's not the case. I feel like any little word out of her mouth will set me off like a rocket and I don't want to spend my energy fighting today. I don't have it in me anymore to argue.

Mom pulls up right around the time that Christopher has fallen asleep in his crib. I take in a deep breath of courage before answering the door. She has flowers in her hand and extends them out to me. Mom's never been a sentimental person, so this surprised yet touched me somewhere deep inside. "Thanks Mom," I say, while guiding her into a hug. "Please come on in. We can talk while we wait for Christopher to wake up," her mouth frowns when she hears he's not awake, but she graciously comes inside.

"Ashley, sweetheart, how are you feeling? I've been over it in my mind again and again on whether to talk to you about this or not, but I have to. Baby, I swear I never would have given you any advice that I thought even for a fraction of a second would harm you or my grand babies. I don't know how I'll ever forgive myself. Are you bonding with Christopher? Mothers who lose one of a set of twins are way more susceptible to postpartum depression," she threw her hands over her mouth instantly. "What am I saying? Of course, you're going to be depressed. I just want to make sure you're able to bond with the baby who's here and not spend all your time missing the one who isn't. He is gonna help you heal sure as anything. You two need each other right now."

It's a bittersweet shock to my heart, but I can't argue her point. They were words I didn't want but really needed to hear. I hold my hand up to pause her for a second politely. "Hang on, I hear the baby crying." I stood up to go into his room. My mother's voice trails behind me, "Ash, I don't hear anything."

When I enter the nursery, I can still see the imprints on the carpet from where the other crib was set up. I try to smooth them out with my foot while my hands smooth the tears from my face. My mom was right, Christopher was sleeping soundly. I heard him crying clear as day, but I guess he fell back asleep before I got in here. I walk back into the kitchen and rejoin my mother at the table.

"It was nothing. I thought he was crying, but I was wrong, he's asleep. He's as happy as a bug in a rug, swaddled up tight." I assured Mom. She chuckles lightly. "That's normal sometimes. You'll think you hear them do all kinds of things. It just means your ears are alert and tuned to your baby. It's the sign of a good mother." We talk for a few more moments and then I hug her goodbye. The rest of the month goes on with lots of these instances. It gets so bad that finally I mention it to the pediatrician at Christopher's two-month appointment. "He just cries so loudly, like he needs something.

And then by the time I get to him, he's either lying peacefully or asleep." I explained to her.

She grins and assures me all is well. "Babies sometimes just make noises, even in their sleep. It can be quite confusing and alarming to some at first, but it's normal. He could be self-soothing himself by the time you reach his room, and that's a really great thing. A sign of a smart baby that will likely grow to be an independent child. Try not to worry about it. You noticing just means you're close to your baby. It's the sign of a good mother." After having said that, she left the room. I packed up our things and went home.

Corey is off today and with these crying instances I didn't sleep well last night at all. "Mama is going to have herself a quick nap." I tell Corey. I hand him our baby and give both my boys a kiss. The instant my head hits the pillow I can feel the pull of sleep sag my periphery and I fade away quickly.

I wake up to the blaring siren of a baby's cry. My feet are on the floor before my eyes are even open. "Alright Chris, Mama's gonna be right there. Hang on okay? I gotta make you a bottle. It's okay. Shhh shhh shhhh." I'm still lovingly shushing in the kitchen after the bottle is made. My phone vibrates and I pick it up off the counter. It's a text message from Corey.

I call out encouragingly to the baby again as I open the message. *Hey baby. You looked really tired today, so I took Chris out with me to get groceries. We should be home in a couple of hours. Enjoy your rest. Love ya!*

Maybe they came back early because Chris was too fussy. The message must have just now come through. Sometimes our phones do that. I turn the corner to Christopher's room, and I still hear the crying, so I'm not too worried. However, the second, and I mean the second, my toe enters the room, the crying stops. Complete silence seeps all around me in its place.

With trepidation, I creep closer to the crib, not wanting to disturb him. Lying there peacefully all safe and sound is.... no one.

It's empty and cold to the touch. The crib is completely and totally empty. I drop to my knees and sob; the tremors coursing through my body faster than my breath can keep up with.

After searching the house and calling Corey, I believe I know what's going on now. When I had told Christopher at birth that his brother was always with him, I didn't realize just how accurate I was. I still have both of my babies. I can't help but wonder about the things William will say when he learns how to talk.

THE RITUAL

I've been a widower for exactly six years now. I was blissfully married to a woman named Ava for fifteen amazing years. We didn't have much in the beginning, but we were happy that way. She always said she'd rather struggle with a man that she absolutely loved than to have luxury with a man she didn't. Ava was good to me that way, never made me feel bad about anything...

Sorry... way, six years ago today she was taken from me. It was February 14th; I wasn't feeling well, and she had gone to the natural food market to get me some tea. Ava always made tea when I was sick, pampered me just like a loving mother would. She was just going down one of the aisles and whoosh, her life snuffed out like a candle's flame.

My wife just dropped dead right there in the spices section. Thirty-four years old, she was healthier than I was. Just like that... one aneurysmal subarachnoid hemorrhage later and she was gone forever.

I've tried to make it on my own, but I can't. Food has no taste, water quenches no thirst and sleep provides no rest, not without Ava. I've prayed to Heaven, to Hell, to anyone that could bring her back. Finally, I resign myself to the wonders of the internet. After days of searching, I finally found something, a kind of ritual. I've nothing to lose and in the worst-case scenario, nothing happens other than I've wasted some time and money.

The items are collected, and the ritual performed. I feel no different after, still just exhausted in every way one's spirit can be. Trying not to get my hopes up, I go to bed. After a fitful sleep, a cold, empty bed greets me in the morning. I guess I really don't expect much difference. Refusing to succumb to my dejection, I surrender myself to my daily routine.

I drove to the store to buy some food for the dog and a pack of smokes; it was the one thing I wasn't able to do when Ava was alive. She hated smoking, especially the smell on my breath. 'ash tray kisses', she'd say.

The day was gorgeous but felt heavy to me for some reason. I guess everything feels heavy these days, though. When your only purpose for the last fifteen years has been to make someone happy, what do you do with yourself now that that purpose is gone?

Halfway through the day, the door makes a strained squeak as I hear it open. I descend the stairs, confused but hopeful.

There she is, my beautiful Ava. She looks amazing, younger than she did when she died, if you could believe that. She places a bag of groceries down on the counter and takes out a box of tea.

"Babe, what happened to the car? I drove it to the store. When I came out it was gone," she explains. "I had to call one of those Uber things. The guy had packs of cheez-its in his car. I got your tea by the way," she kisses my cheek and pauses. "Hey, Matty... did you do something different with the house? It looks so gloomy in here. Open some shit up, come on. Let some light in. Wait... were you smoking? Yeah, open the door but leave the screen closed," she flirtatiously glares at me, then proceeds to flit about the house, cleaning and arranging like no years have passed at all.

Cautiously I walk up to her and touch her face, half expecting my hand to pass right through her. It doesn't though. Her warm face nuzzles into the groove of my hand and her eyes close, absorbing the love of my touch.

I hug her fiercely and we made love like we hadn't in years, literally. I can't stop staring at her. My heart is so caught up in the relief from its torment that I can't bring myself to question everything now. Let me enjoy this first, doubt can come tomorrow.

Twelve hours have passed and suddenly Ava screams! Her bones contort and her eyes freeze over. She clutches her heart and drops off of the bed, rigid by the time she hits the ground. I faint, wake up and it's morning again. Ava is laying there on her side smiling at me with no recollection of the night before.

That first morning I rushed her to the doctor, explaining what I saw the previous night. They both stare at me with bewildered faces. Ava swears to him that she feels fine and suggests that maybe I'm the one who needs to be checked out. As if this was the time for jokes, I watched her die! After everything comes back normal, he sends us home. But not before giving me a list of recommended therapists that accept our insurance.

The rest of the week continues. Other than being a little more withdrawn due to plaguing images of a dying wife, things are great. I started to enjoy her more and more; my suspicion shrinking smaller and smaller every day that went by. After all, this is what I prayed for. She's back in my life, she didn't come back a rotted corpse, she's not full of evil carried over 'from the other side', she's just Ava.

It was exactly one week to the day that she'd returned when I'm robbed of my security. The catch to my bargain was like the hand of death gripping at my throat.

We're out driving and decide to pull over and go for a walk. The sky is just beginning to fill with the colors of the fading sun. Ava drops her phone on the sidewalk. When I bend to retrieve it, she moves over to allow me room to do so. Just then, a truck swerves to avoid something large in the roadway and Ava is hit.

"Matty, I love you!" she cries out, seconds before impact. I see the beautiful blue of her eyes get lighter and lighter as her life fades. The crimson pool surrounding her blends in with her auburn hair.

I call for an ambulance and hold my love as I wait for help, even though I know there is none. Nothing can help her now but the sweet release of the afterlife. They take her away and I sob hard. You would think the agony of seeing my wife die for the third time would take on an almost surreal kind of element to it.

However, it becomes more and more devastating each time that it happens. Am I in Hell? It feels that way, but I haven't really done anything in my life to deserve such a fate. Not to mention I'm most definitively sure I'm not dead. My pounding headaches and constant sweat-stained nightmares make me sure of that.

I awake the next morning once again to the chill of a cold, empty bed. This time though, I smell bacon. I can hear Ava's lovingly tone-deaf voice singing from the kitchen.

"All you gotta do is, man, hold her when you wanna squeeze her, don't tease her, never leave her. Get to her, got, got, got to try a little tenderness," I smile as I recognize her favorite song.

However, as much as I want to rush to her, hold her and join in the song; I cannot move. My mind has a moment of true insanity. Like the kind where you don't know if you're in a dream or you keep dreaming about waking up from a dream, but you're in another dream. It's madness. My mind shuts down as I struggle to sort out reality from its alternative. I continue to lay there motionless in a pool of sickly-sweet smelling sweat.

Week after week she leaves me, all in different ways. It seems like the more I try to keep her safe, the more violent her deaths become. She chokes on a homemade dinner I make her the first week of September. She's struck down by a seizure that causes cardiac arrest the middle week of October. The third of December I thought I finally beat it! She lays down next to me and just falls asleep. There was no blood, no screams, no demons taking over her body movements, just sleep.

I left to take some medicine and when I came back, she was still there. I get so excited. I actually jump up and down with joy until I see that her eyes are open. They are fixed in a lifeless thousand-yard stare, the irises almost a blue-white. Again, she is gone. So, I lay there and held her body until the morning breathed life back into it. I know the marble cold skin will be replaced by warm breathing silk by the time I wake up again.

Ashamedly after about the sixteenth week in a fit of insanity, I killed her myself. In the most respectfully loving way possible if there even is such a thing. The look in her eyes as she realizes what I've done was worse than any death I had seen thus far. I think that look will stick with me the most. I see it in her smile, when we make love, when she cries at something beautiful. I just wanted to change it, break the cycle. I'd try anything. But she would die and then be vibrant and beautiful the next morning like nothing happened, over and over again.

The cliche'd phrase 'careful what you wish for' plays through my brain like a broken record. You tell me, is it worth it? Would you be able to handle the mental anguish over and over again just to have one more day? The same day with different events, all leading to the one your love's death.

I have nightmares of waking up next to her rotted face.

"Till death do us part Matty," she says as her lower lip falls into my lap.

———

It's been almost a year now since it started. I'm rapidly losing my mind. How many times do I have to watch this? As if once didn't burn it into my every thought. It will always be the last thing I see before I go to sleep and the first thing I think about in the morning. Her image is perverting to me. Her eyes are starting to look the same alive as they do when she's dead...

LEGOS

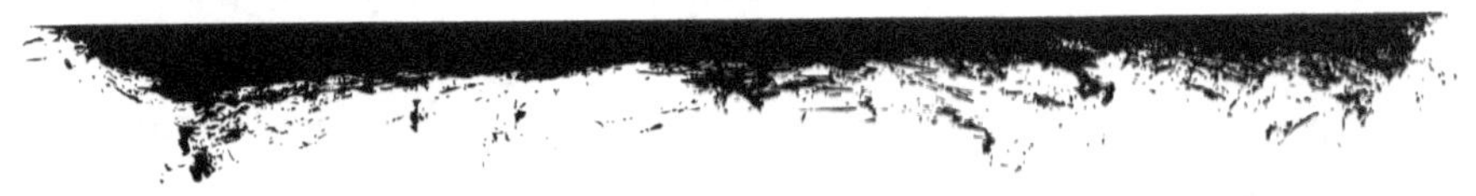

I really... really hate Legos. The little nubs and sharp corners that fit perfectly right into the center of the bottom of your foot, causing a stabbing agony that lingers for the rest of the day with every step.

My son and I woke up forty-five minutes late this morning. The very first thing I see upon opening my bedroom door is a hardwood minefield of discarded Legos in the hallway. I step over most of them gingerly but my impatience with getting a move on gets the best of me. The second to last Lego impales the arch of my foot, assaulting my nerve endings with a lightning bolt of pain.

Through gritted teeth I wake up my son and help him rush to get ready for school. I prepare the coffee maker and get all the way to the last step when I mournfully realize I'm out of drinking water. My kiddo gets on his bus, I get in my car, and we go our separate ways for the day.

I grab a lukewarm, unsatisfying cup of coffee at a drive through café and continue to drive to work. Things should all be better once I get there. That promotion is as good as mine. I've already started spending my sign-on bonus already. I'll be so happy and proud to tell my son that his Daddy got the job.

He deserves a better life and nice things. He barely ever asks me for anything and is so appreciative, even at his young age, of every gift he receives. I think I'm going to take him to the theme park two towns over that he loves. We've only been able to go once, and it rained the whole day. He loved it, though. My boy smiled ear to ear through the whole park, wetter than a drowned rat, but as happy as a June bug.

I pull into the parking lot and walk inside the building. My confidence soars with every slightly pained step forward that I take towards the conference room. It looks like most of the office is already inside. Quite a few heads turn my way to greet me with warm smiles as I take my seat at the conference table.

"Alright everyone. Now that Reinhardt's here we can get on with business," he gives me a wink of comradery after saying my last name. I take the subtlest of deep breaths as I mentally prepare myself for a victorious acceptance platitude. I need to be prepared to humbly respond to the impending promotion announcement.

My boss continues. "As you are all aware, a promotion became available last month. After carefully going over performance reviews and customer satisfaction rates, we've finally chosen the perfect candidate. Please give a warm welcome to your new assistant director..." I rise to my feet and brush off the sides of my suit jacket as the name falls from his lips into the atmosphere. "...Stewart Brown." A middle-aged man in the back of the room also has risen to his feet and with an accomplished, proud smile on his face.

My hands unconsciously come together and start clapping to join the others in the room. I force a thin smile across my lips as my eyes meet Stewart's. I give a congratulatory nod. My feet guide me in betrayal as I find myself walking towards him. I shake his hand with as much positivity as I can muster, secretly loathing that this man got the job that should have rightfully been mine.

As soon as it's time for my lunch break, I step outside to call my wife. I really need her loving voice right now. The sinking fear that she will leave me for my shortcoming's nags at my mind. She's not that kind of woman, though. It's just the voice in my head, the voice that I never want to listen to but is the one that never goes away.

Only popping up when I'm feeling my highest, or lowest. Talking to my wife always makes me feel better, I love her so much.

Her phone rings only once and then directs me to voicemail. I dial the number again, seeking the much—needed relief that her presence always gives me. However, the result is the same. I decided to call her on her work line, figuring she was just getting back from her break by now. This time, a woman's voice answers on the third ring. "Thank you for calling the Harper and Stone Realty Office! This is Sherrie, how can I help you today?" Confusedly, I answered her. "Uhh... yeah hi Sherrie. May I please speak to Anna Reinhardt? This is her husband, Gerald."

For a moment, only silence greets me on the other end of the line. Finally, Sherrie answers, her voice small and dripping with wariness. "I'm sorry Mr. Reinhardt; I hate to be the one to tell you this. Anna hasn't worked here for the past two weeks. She got some paperwork mixed up that caused us to lose an extremely large sale. We had no choice... unfortunately, she had to be let go." I murmur a thank you and dejectedly hang up the phone.

A million sharp needles impale my temples with the first signs of an oncoming migraine. I've suffered from them for the past few years. They are heavily aggravated, if not solely caused, by stress. Of all the things that I've encountered today, this is truly the last thing I need. My foot throbs with pain with every step I take back towards my office.

The workday drags on and it seems to take forever to end. When it does, I am only too relieved to leave the building and start my commute home. My wife and I have a lot to talk about with her lying about still working at her job.

Caught up in the eagerness of arriving home, I almost forget to stop and get milk and eggs from the grocery store. I want to make my son a warm breakfast tomorrow to make up for the shitty pop tart he ate in his rush to be on time this morning. The lines aren't too long and I'm in and out in under twenty minutes. The pain in my temples starts to ease. Something finally seems to be going my way. Thank God too, I was about to lose it.

My feet shuffle out into the parking lot. Suddenly the eggs fall to the ground... followed by the sound of twelve fatal cracks. Right there, not thirty feet away from me, is my car. Someone had decided to relocate my mirror for me as well as give me an exceptionally large decorative dent to my driver door. How fucking nice of them! The full force of my migraine hits like a tidal wave against the white pavement as I stumble closer to assess the damage, the pain in my foot having increased in intensity enough to cause a slight limp at this point.

On closer inspection, I now see it's not a dent on my door but a huge gash. There's no way that's going to buff or pound out. Maybe there's a note? Nope, of course not... That would have been too easy, right? I don't know how much more of this I can take. Murphy's Law is having its way with me today and without a prophylactic to boot. My mind feels like a thin wire stretched to its very limits; any little event causing it to SNAP.

An empty driveway greets me when I arrive home. No surprise there, I guess. Anna still has an hour before she's due home from wherever it is that she's going that's NOT work.

I exit my car just in time to see my boy get off the school bus. His little face wears a look of consternation as he sets his book bag down inside and flops on the couch. First grade's tough on him, I guess. He looks like a little man who just had the same kinda day that I did at work today.

After dinner, I take him upstairs to get ready for a bath. He absolutely hates them, and I find myself once again trying to mentally prepare for an unfortunate situation. I hear the cordless phone start to ring and close my eyes with discouragement as I remember I left it downstairs. My guy's a big boy, but certainly not old enough to be left unsupervised near a tub filling rapidly with water. So, I let it ring. If it's important, the machine will get it.

I hear Anna's voice on the recorded greeting and the telltale beep. "Hey honey! I am soooo sorry but I'm gonna be *super* late coming home tonight. Things got crazy today at work with this new housing development and I have to stay late to catch up. I have no idea how long it will take. Don't wait up ok? I'll wake you up when I get home. Can't wait to hear about your promotion today! Love you!"

The words sink in, and I feel my left eye start to twitch. Before long, it feels like half of the side of my face is quaking with misfiring nerve endings. My son comes out of his room, hears the water, and starts to wail in protest. My head feels like it's being split in two. It's agonizing to keep my eyes open and the now excruciating pain in my foot reverberates with every heartbeat.

I woke up late, stepped on a Lego, had to rush to leave the house, didn't get the promotion today, my wife has been lying to me for two weeks about work, someone smashed the side of my car, I have a migraine from hell, the house is a mess, my wife is out somewhere unknown till an unknown time, my son is screaming, and my foot hurts.

My son's tantrum reaches a new pitch that shoots a shock of pain into my cerebellum like a bullet. I tell him to calm down and stop, but he won't lower his wailing enough to hear me. I plead with him, hot tears pricking my eyes to stop, to please be quiet for Daddy for just a minute.

I turn to take a step into the hallway towards him and my peripheral vision blurs with white light. It takes about two seconds for the pain to register that I have stepped on yet another Lego, this one a sharp piece to a mountain top. Effectively puncturing the skin of my foot and drawing blood in the process. My eyes widen and my hands fly out to steady myself. My arm comes into contact with a solid force long enough to regain my bearings.

I woke up late, stepped on a Lego, had to rush to leave the house, didn't get the promotion today, my wife has been lying to me for two weeks about work, someone smashed the side of my car, I have a migraine from hell, the house is a mess, my wife is out somewhere unknown till an unknown time, my son is screaming, and now... my foot really fucking hurts.

My head... my foot... the damn Legos.

I stepped on a Lego. The hallway was full of Legos. We woke up late this morning... we rushed to leave the house...

The hallway was full of Legos... we woke up late this morning... we rushed to leave the house... I stepped on yet another damned Lego... my foot is bleeding... my hands fly out to steady myself.

The hallway... was full... of Legos... We woke up late this morning... we rushed to leave the house... I stepped on yet another damned Lego... my foot is bleeding. My hands fly out to steady myself... My arm came into contact with a solid force....

And *my son's body lies lifeless and broken at the* bottom of the stairs.

FOREVER HALLOWEEN

There were only a dozen or more houses on our street, and only two of them have families with children. Chuck Murphy has twin boys named Aaron and Bryan. They're seven years old and creepily well behaved for kids their age. I imagine at one time there was a Mrs. Murphy, but she's certainly nowhere to be found now. Then there's us, the Hull family. My wife Bianca and I have a daughter, Caprice, who is a ten-year-old bundle of curiosity and intelligence. Our not so little girl, who just six years ago wanted to be a pink princess for Halloween, is going as a Necromancer this year. One hooded cloak, dress, a skull pendant and dark lipstick later, and she was good to go.

We normally went trick or treating together. Bianca is working late at the emergency veterinary clinic and Caprice is more than old enough to walk at the front of the group, so I decide to hang back with Chuck and shoot the shit. His boys' costumes were very well put together. Aaron's wearing a vampire's cloak. His hair's slicked back with what smells like baby oil and two fangs are perched over his front canines. Bryan's wrapped head to toe in tattered gauze, spending his evening as an Egyptian mummy.

They receive quite the haul, with there being only a dozen or so houses on our street. Our weary-footed, sleepy-eyed children trudged back to their houses, bulging bags of candy dragging a bare trail through the dirt and leaves.

It wasn't until seven o'clock the next morning that we heard the screaming.

Caprice flies down the stairs from her bedroom, eyes wild with alarm and concern. "What's going on?" She asks dismissively, running past her mother and I out the front door.

"WAIT!" I shout, to no avail.

Chuck is screaming in agony in his front yard. Two small, broken bodies lay before him. Bryan, the smaller of the two, looks like his body's centuries old. Tattered scraps of discarded gauze flap around his dust infested face. Aaron's body is charred, still smoldering with acrid smelling smoke.

"Holy shit Chuck!" I scream. "What the hell happened here?"

"Their costumes..." he wails. "Bryan fell asleep in his costume. By the time we tried to take it off this morning, he turned to fucking dust! His blood evaporated right in my hands, Jared." I kneel down to console him, trying to hide the sickening in my gut from the smell.

"Aaron..." he continues, "My boy burst into flames the second he went out in the sun."

I look at Caprice and Bianca, mortified and heartbroken. Caprice surprisingly steps forward. She places her hands on the dead bodies, impervious to the heat of Aaron's burning flesh. Her eyes turn white and begin to glow.

She collapses in exhaustion as Bryan's brittle bones rise and fall to the ground. "I tried Daddy, but it's too late," she sobs.

CANDY SNATCHER

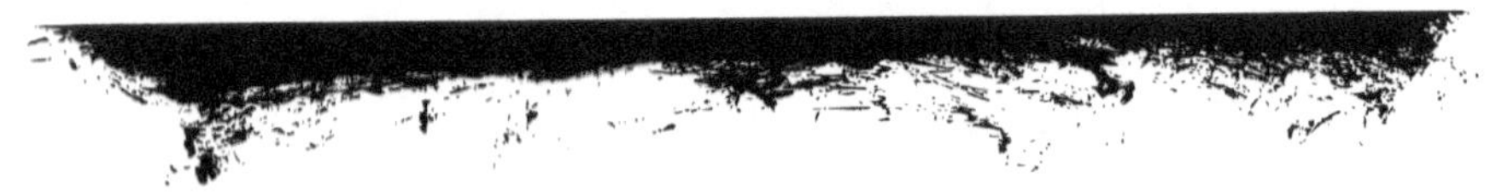

Halloween. Yeah, I don't celebrate that day anymore. That's the day that ruined my life. Now I know what you're thinking; maybe somebody snatched my candy bag as a kid and soured me on the holiday, maybe the cute girl at the Halloween party shut me down... forever altering my confidence. But it wasn't anything like that. This was something real; something far worse... pure evil.

When I was fourteen or so, a couple buddies and my girlfriend Hannah showed up at my back window. They wanted me to go out with them. My parents were so busy screaming at each other that they didn't care that I was even there, much less have any objections to my absence. I could have gone out the front door if I wanted, to be honest. But it was more fun to sneak out. Even if my jaw was throbbing.

The arrival of colder weather brought the worst out of my broken tooth. I'd been lying to my mother about it to avoid the dentist and having to miss school. My girlfriend was in an after-school club with me. It was our only chance to be together for more than just five minutes here and there between classes.

The night air was cool and damp. It felt good on my skin, like liberation. Considering what my friends had in mind, that's honestly the most appropriate word for it. Plenty of children would be liberated from their candy bags tonight.

See, we were candy snatchers, punks, the ruiner of fun for little children. We told ourselves at the time that any kid out that late had it coming. Eddie would say, "It wasn't our fault they were in the right place at the wrong time".

Besides, everyone knew that Halloween candy got marked down 75% at all the stores the next day, anyway.

It never fails. Sympathetic parents will buy candy by the droves to satisfy a broken-hearted child. Those kids made bank because of us. At least that's what we thought... that's what I told myself the year before. I'll tell ya what though, I saw those kids crying every time I closed my eyes until Thanksgiving.

I swore to myself I wouldn't ever do it again, but my parents had me feeling some kind of way. There was anger. Anger I didn't understand much less know how to express rationally. Destruction was instant gratification; it fueled my needs.

Now, we weren't bad kids. Bag-grabbing was the most homeless crime kids our age could have been up to that night. The rest were out partying, drinking, driving, or vandalizing. We weren't in the woods drunk with some girls' legs up in the air. We cruised around the streets, hanging out and listening to music. Sure, there may have been a joint or two, but that was commonplace back then.

We weren't in the car for fifteen minutes when we saw them; four little kids all dressed in the same costume. It was the weirdest thing I'd ever seen. They wore red robes with devil horns and a red mask that covered only the area around their eyes.

Their heights told me they were various ages. It was probably some bored mother's idea. She likely made the matching outfits for her kids.

I almost felt sorry for them at first, to be honest. They just stood there without emotion. Those kids had to have heard us coming, though none looked in our direction. There was barely any reaction when we grabbed their bags, no sadness or outrage, just blank stares on their faces. It wasn't until I started to drive away that any movement occurred. As I looked out the back window, all four of their heads snapped up in our direction.

I was no expert, but I was certain that I'd never seen any kids like these before. Their eyes glowed red all at once, like they were caught in an eternal camera flash.

That was the only movement their bodies emitted. It didn't even look like they were breathing. There were no puffs of warmth in the cold night air, no rising of shoulders as they inhaled breath, nothing.

Glowing eyes, like hot coals, stayed visible through the fog, long after their forms fell away into the shadows of distance. Chills wrapped around my bones, one by one. They settled there. No matter how much I hugged myself to create a rise in temperature. My head felt heavy, so I closed my eyes. The children's retinas burned into my subconscious.

We got to my house not long after. Our hauls were poured into the middle of the floor; each person took what they liked. In no time at all, we were smoking in a rotation and an eighth of the candy was gone. I tried my luck with a kit kat bar, bad move. Bursts of agony shot into my left ear and temple like a knitting needle. Clumps of chocolate peppered the sink as I spit out the candy. Warm salt water soothed my tooth like a warm blanket.

A clatter from the living room cut my relief short. It sounded like someone broke something; that's all I needed at the moment. It felt like the side of my face was kicked by a donkey, and now people were breaking stuff. Greatttt.

Hannah was screaming my name repeatedly; someone else was yelling to call for an ambulance. The scene before me was pure chaos.

Those sounds I heard belonged to Eddie's body as it fell to the floor. His bones twisted and creaked with convulsions. Crimson and brown foam bubbled forth from the depths of his throat, and his eyes were fixed on something within his skull that we could not see. His turbulent heartbeat turned erratic, before quickly stopping altogether.

Hannah was soon to follow. Her death coming swifter and more graceful than Eddie's. She hadn't eaten nearly as much candy as he did. The last words she uttered on this earth were about children.

"The children... why are they laughing?"

Burning pains consumed my torso, bringing me to my knees with pain. The wind was knocked out of me as my body slumped to the floor. It wasn't fair, I didn't even fully eat one single piece of candy. Tinkling squeaks reverberated off the walls of my living room. I understood what Hannah meant then. The last thing I heard before my consciousness was robbed from me completely, was the ethereal sound of kids laughing.

I came to in a hospital bed. A charcoal treatment saved my life but also left me with mental disturbances that I'll never be rid of. Whenever I'm around a fire, I'm still convinced I can taste it. But perhaps that's just my burden to bear.

Maybe that's just what happens when you steal candy from children, especially demonic ones.

THE INFLATABLE SANTA

I had just about finished the genitals on the gingerbread man when my husband's voice boomed through the kitchen, making me slip and leaving one particular cookie way more endowed than he had any right to be.

What? Y'all don't make yours anatomical? It's a naughty little Christmas tradition we started since we have no children. Don't act like you don't do it or know someone who has.

Anyway, Mike was beyond mad at whatever the hell he was going on about in the other room. I stifled a sigh and gave myself permission for a quick eye roll before entering the living room.

"The fucking Browns... Do you see this, Helen?" he asked; frantically gesturing to our front window.

No response entered my mind or left my lips, as I knew I wouldn't need one.

"This is a tiny, boxed in cul-de-sac. There isn't room for half of the holiday shit he puts up. And this new one..." He pauses to let out a scoff. "This takes the cake."

Across the street sat Mary and George Brown. They were the sweetest older couple; never hurt or bothered anybody. But for some reason, they represented every insecurity my husband had about himself. He was never too rude or hateful to their face, but only because I bore the brunt of his verbal diarrhea behind their backs.

An inflatable Santa Claus consumed most of the entrance to their front yard; like ten pounds of leaves crammed into an eight-pound trash bag.

"They even parked their car on the street to make room for it!" Mike prattled on.

The tinny chime of our doorbell interrupted his tirade. My gratitude for a temporary escape sped my steps to the door.

Mrs. Brown's rosy face greeted me from our front porch.

"Hello Mrs. Brown! Would you like a cookie? I have some freshly made in the kitchen."

My manners completely made me forget the fact that they were naughty gingerbread cookies; tits and all. I was all too relieved when she declined.

Proverbial sparkles danced in the corners of her eyes as she smiled up at me.

"George and I are going out of town to see our boys for the Christmas holiday; back home to West Virginia, where we're from. We leave tomorrow morning and we'll be back by Sunday evening if the weather permits. Do you have any plans, dear?" She asked. I could tell she was hopeful for a certain answer, but which one I wasn't sure yet.

"Nope, not really. We're just gonna buy a premade turkey from Publix and open gifts before bed on Christmas Eve. My family came down sick this holiday, so we are going to reconvene in January when everyone's feeling better."

An audible sigh of relief escaped her thin lips. "That's too bad about your folks, hunny. But would it be any trouble for one of you to collect the mail and maybe shovel the walk the day before we're due back? I'll be happy to pay you for your troubles." Mary explained.

Mike wasn't going to be happy, but when an adorable little lady asks you to help her, what kind of person would I be to say no? We had to shovel ours anyway and well, theirs was just across the way. Hell, I'll do it myself if he doesn't want to.

"Of course, Mrs. Brown. We'd be happy to, no payment necessary. You guys just have fun on your trip, okay? If you really want to pay me, bring me back some pepperoni rolls, yeah?" I winked.

She chuckled, agreed and told us to have a Merry Christmas as she left the front porch. I watched as her aging frame shuffled across our yard and into hers, stopping to brush some loose snow off the Santa Claus before going inside. At first, I thought Mike was just being an asshole; but the thing really is grotesquely huge.

My husband had overheard the entire exchange and is now eyeing me furiously.

"Aren't there enough things that you ask me to do *here at home?*"

I cut him off at the pass. "Yeah, I know. It's really no big deal, okay?"

"How long are they gonna be gone?"

"Only five days. She's gonna bring back pepp rolls. It's gonna be fine."

Mike's eyes took on a glint of mischief as inhaled to speak. "So... do you think they'll deflate Santa before they go?"

"What the fu-"

"If they don't, can I do it?" He interrupted.

At this point, I just wanted it all to be over with. The last thing I wanted to incur was another one of his rants. The negativity takes layers off of one's life, I just know it does. So, I agreed.

"If they don't deflate it, you can let the air out of the damn thing. As long as you don't damage it... I don't care. But you're shoveling that walk!"

The next morning came and went. We waved the Browns off as they drove away. The Santa Claus loomed in their wake, swaying tauntingly at my husband. It was almost funny, really; I can remember giggling despite the anger I felt boiling in his chest.

"Don't be upset. You get to deflate it, remember?

Give it one hour and-"

Mike was already across the lawn, heading into their yard. It really was amazing how long those things take to fully deflate. We watched it from our front window. It was sad, like watching the wicked warlock of the North Pole. It just melted into itself until it was nothing but a nylon puddle in their front yard.

I spent the rest of the day researching the internet. That's what it's there for right? Seriously though, I had no idea how to re-inflate that thing by the time they got home. I wasn't sure if it needed a pump or if there was a button you pushed. Mike was completely unsympathetic to my concern.

"We'll just tell them that it was really windy here one day, so I deflated it to prevent it from being damaged. Problem solved. It's better than my initial plan of stabbing a hole in it with a shovel and saying it was an accident."

Unbelievable.

The welcoming smell of coffee didn't wake me the next day, nor the morning sun shining through the windows. It was the sound of my husband yelling in the kitchen.

"What the hell is this?!?" He was gesturing frantically once again toward our front window. "I can't fucking believe this!"

The Santa Claus stood proud and victorious on their front lawn as if nothing ever changed. I couldn't believe my eyes.

"Maybe it's on a timer?" I muttered uselessly.

My shoulder knocked back against the wall as I backed out of his way. His eyes were menacingly wide, and his features were set hard; it looked like they had never seen a day of joy. A clatter came from inside the kitchen as he rummaged through the dishwasher.

"Mike, hey... what are you doing?" My voice came out high pitched, but even toned. Getting angry hadn't ever done me any good when he got like that.

He emerged with a kitchen knife, one of the sharpest that we've had.

"That windstorm," He breathed through huffs. "Maybe it blew a tree branch into their Santa and I didn't notice it until I was shoveling the walk."

Those poor people! I really shouldn't joke about such things, but maybe I should increase my knowledge of divorce law for my new year's resolution.

A scream cut through the cold air, lingering to muffle through the windowpanes before reaching my ears. I began to run to the front door as fast as my feet would take me. On my way out, I glanced at the window.

The neighbor's front yard was a smattering of crimson against the white of freshly fallen snow. My husband lay gurgling in the street by their mailbox. I pulled out my phone and dialed 911. As I looked up from the screen, the Santa was moving.

A figure dressed in black erupted from the middle of the Santa suit, bleeding profusely from the stomach. He left trails of blood throughout the snow as he ran off through their backyard.

The police came in no time at all; apprehending and calling an ambulance for the man that had now killed my husband. It turned out he had been casing their house for a couple of weeks. He knew they'd be going on vacation and depended on the cover of the inflatable to hide himself until nightfall. The robber survived his injuries and fully served out a five-year sentence in a prison the next county over. Five years... that's all he got for ruining my life.

Christmas will never be the same to me. I've since remarried during that time, and we now have a three-year-old daughter. A chill goes up my spine every time we see an inflatable Christmas decoration.

And what's worse, our neighbor just put up the largest inflatable snowman I've ever seen across the street.

LIST OF GRIEVANCES

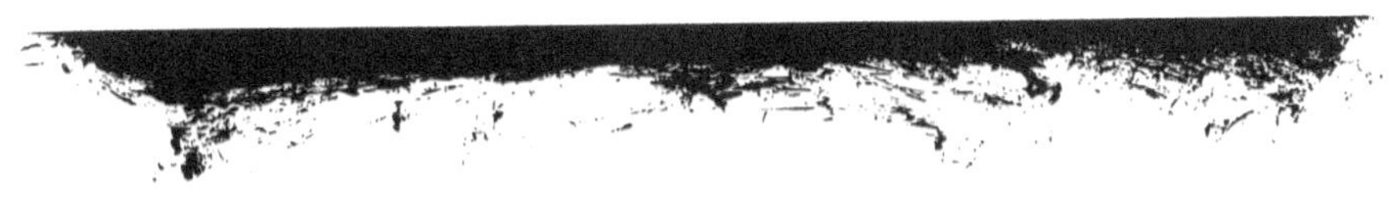

I've been in therapy for anger management for the past six months now. No, I didn't hulk out and get arrested for battery or anything like that. My husband sought out therapy for me due to me snapping all the time.

It's my go to. My mind is always so caught up in trying to right itself. It's a jumbled knot of doubts, insecurities, and fears. Each time I stop and try to even attempt to straighten and separate that knot into rational and irrational pathways, our son Martin interrupts me, sending the thoughts back into their nest of dread like a startled turtle. Questions are too much to bear at times. There have been plenty of instances where he's tried to get my attention and I've snapped at him, only for him to have wanted to show me a picture he drew for me.

With all of my heart, I can assure you that I don't want to be this way. My husband Josh and I had an extremely hard time getting pregnant with Martin. It took us four years and two miscarriages. It sickens me to have given birth to this beautiful, healthy child only to snap at him all the time.

Anyway, that's my deal. My therapist told me to start writing things down and, well... I kinda got addicted to it.

"When one of those vile, intrusive thoughts enters your mind, treat them as if they were leaves floating on a stream. Briefly acknowledge them, then let them float on by until they disappear. Don't try to hold on to one for too long. And the ones that are too large to float, write them down. Especially anger; get it on paper and out of your heart. If someone makes you mad or hurts you, write them a letter. You don't even have to give it to them. The act alone will make you feel better."

Those were his exact words.

Today is the day that Martin and I go to the local mall to see Santa. The line's impossibly long; weaving in and out of the aisles like the frayed ends of my hair. I have to remind myself that even though Martin was three and likely won't remember this, it's an investment for his future. It means a lot to me as a mother to have these memories with him. He will only be little like this once.

It would be so much easier if Josh was here with us. He's been working two jobs to ensure the best Christmas possible for our little family. That's what I tell myself, at least. In reality... I feel like a single parent, as shitty as that is to say, and that I have to do everything concerning Martin on my own.

But I paste a smile on my weather numbed face and wait in line with my little guy, like a good mom. Martin's hand is squirming around like an electric eel in a frying pan. One step out and the people behind us would bumrush us out of line. And I really don't want to have to punch someone in the face today.

When it's finally our turn, store employee elves lift little Martin onto Santa's lap, pausing just long enough for pictures. It takes my most embarrassing efforts to get him to cooperate with Santa long enough to get a decent one. He rattles off a lengthy list, appropriately creative for a little dude his age. An elf presents him with a candy cane as he hops off Santa's lap. I thank him and turn around to leave.

"Ho. Ho. Ho. And what would you like for Christmas this year, Mommy?" 'Santa' asks, stopping me in my tracks.

As this happens, Martin drops his freshly unwrapped candy cane on the floor, initiating a siren of tears. The man playing Santa still stares at me expectantly despite the display. Can't he see how badly I want to leave? There are a lot of people behind us, and I can already hear sighs of annoyance as an unknown voice from towards the back of the line drifts up to us.

"See Bonnie? Naughty children don't get presents from Santa. Don't be like that little boy, okay hunny?"

Jesus H. Christ... what a douche.

I sputtered the first thing that came to mind, "I'm good, thank you Santa. Have a Merry Christmas." And rush Martin away from the line.

There's a little play area in the lobby next door with cookies and a make your own ornament station with a sign that has "Santa's Workshop" painted on in large, green glitter letters. Next to it sits a square mailbox with pencils and paper laid out on a table underneath it. It seems kind of redundant since the kids literally just got done telling him what their wish lists are, but I guess it's cute to be able to have something to save.

Martin waddles over to the mailbox right away and knocks all of the pencils off the table. Of course he does. My frustration is boiling, but instead of lashing out at Martin, I engage him in an activity. If he's focused, I can focus. We toddle back over to the table together and I hand him a pencil as I take one myself.

He repeats the list he made for Santa as I write it down. Once he's finished, I tell him to take his pencil and draw Santa a picture as I decide to write my own note.

Dear Santa,

This year, I just... want... peace. I wanna wake up in the morning in silence, if only for ten minutes. I want to go sit on the toilet in peace... without interruption, I want to sleep in until noon like I did before I had kids, I want to have a life again. Can you do that for me? Didn't think so.

Signed—One Exhausted Mother

Martin drew Santa a picture of a squiggly cat with five eyes. I giggle as I fold the piece of paper to stuff in the envelope.

Another mother comes over and asks about enrollment for PreK. I stifle the urge to tell her to calm her tits, and that enrollment isn't until May, but I smile and answer the question. The sooner I'm done with this one, final interaction, the sooner I can go home. It will be overwhelmingly soothing to go from a crowd of dozens of people to just Martin and me. It feels suffocating sometimes.

It's later in the evening now, things are settled and Martin's asleep in his warm bed.

I found the pants I was wearing earlier. A folded square of paper is retrieved from the pocket and placed on my dresser as I leave the room to throw them in the wash. I hate it when paper gets washed. It breaks into those endless little bits. You'll get them all back from the lint trap if you're lucky enough to have it transfer to the drier and not get stuck in the washer drain.

Josh gets off from his second job soon and I want to take a nap to be fresh when he comes home. The time after work where we talk about our days is sometimes the only alone time we have together. We both look forward to it all day.

Martin left one of his blankets on our bed from earlier in the day. I inhale his sweet little boy smell, feeling a tear slip down my face as I remember the letter I wrote to Santa earlier. My sorrows lull me to sleep quickly.

I'm surprised to find the sun shining through our bedroom window when I wake. Martin must be sleeping in. Normally he's tearing through the house before the sun even thinks to rise.

The clock on my bedside reads 11:17AM.

I ran to Martin's room, only to find a storage room. The presents Josh and I put under the tree for him the night before are gone. No discarded toys stab my feet as I walk next to the tree. What's worse, every single handmade ornament we have ever made with Martin is gone.

I run sobbing to our bedroom, throwing open the door. The folded note is still on our dresser. My hands shake as I begin to open it. Horror grips my sense as I see it's not the note I wrote, but the one I wrote for Martin. His squiggle cat still danced across the side of the page.

Violently, I start to shake my husband awake. "Joshua!" I screech through tears. "Where's the baby? What happened to Martin?!?"

My husband stares vacantly through sleepy eyes.

His lips hold a tone of concern as he asks, "Babe... who's Martin?"

THE SECOND NOEL

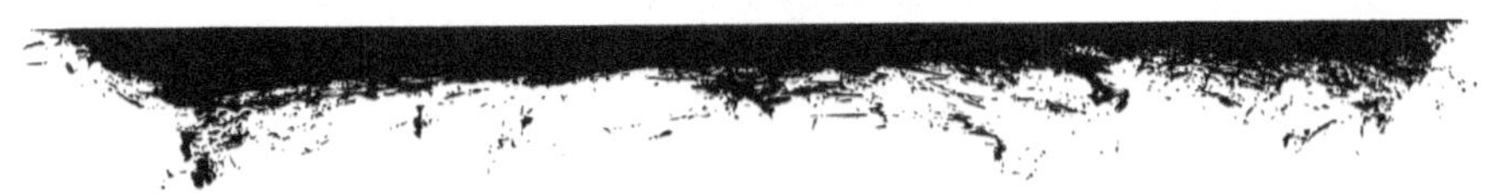

We were careful; so diligent to make sure all candy and sweets were put away before bedtime. The Gingerbread house we made together the night before was placed in the highest cupboard in the house, well out of a five-year-old's reach.

The usual clatter of our Daughter Noel's footsteps and exclamations about presents never came that Christmas morning. Instead, my wife Maureen and I were met with dead silence. A sinister aura permeated through the air.

Two green monster slippers twitched in different directions; a signal of our little girl's struggle with whatever had caused her to fall to the kitchen floor.

"Noel?" No answer.

My wife ran over to her and crouched down on the floor.

"Bobby!" She wailed. "She's choking! Oh my god, her lips are turning blue."

I had her off the floor and well into the first steps of the Heimlich maneuver in less than twenty seconds. All the while, Maureen's sobbing hysterically in my ear.

"Bob, no! You're not supposed to do it like that. She's too little; you're gonna hurt her ribs!"

In the adrenaline of the situation, I find myself shouting back. My hands are shaking so badly that I can barely keep them grasped together under her tiny frame. I'd say my heart was beating faster than my breath could keep up with, if I couldn't feel it shattering more every second that Noel didn't take a breath.

"I'm trying to save our daughter's life! Ribs won't matter if I don't clear this airway in the next thirty seconds. God knows how long she's been out here like this!"

Maureen fumbles through her purse and the contents of the clusterfuck that is our kitchen counter, searching for her phone to call 911.

"Lift her up by the feet and pound her back, Bob!" She demands.

The moment I go to respond, a sharp, jagged shard of something flies into my left eye. My right eye watches as it falls to my lap and rolls to the very floor I picked Noel up off of not moments ago, a fucking peppermint. Our little girl almost lost her life over a goddamned peppermint. We had used them to decorate the roof; Santa's shingles Noel called them. One must have rolled off when we were putting it away last night.

Noel's face goes through a barrage of colors until it returns to its usual pink state. She's coughing quite a bit. Maureen and I are both crying at this point; clutching our daughter to our chests like she'd float away if we ever let go.

"Jesus Christ, sweetheart, you really scared us. Can you breathe okay?"

Our little darling nodded her head.

"Are you sure?" Maureen asked. Pulling her in for an even tighter hug before giving her a chance to answer. "I love you Noel."

She pulls away from us. Her face looks the same as our little girl's always has, but her eyes are oddly different. There's a subtle change that I can't place. As she opens her tiny mouth to speak, her irises turn black. The voice that follows comes out in a deep, menacing rumble.

"Noel isn't here anymore."

THE REAPPEARANCE OF THE BRIGANTINE CHILDREN

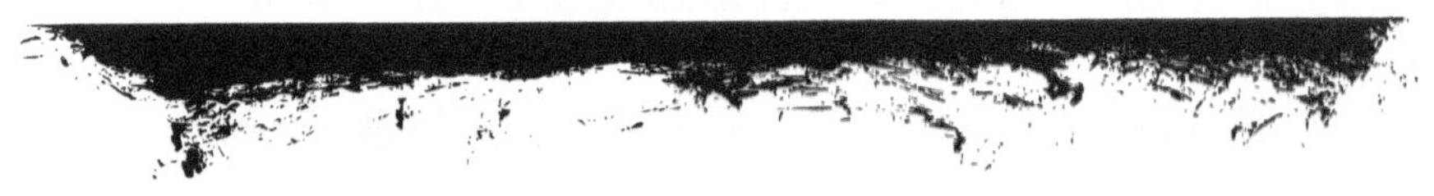

December 25th, 2018, was the worst day our town of Brigantine had seen since its founding. People call it the Christmas of the Lost. My heart still stammers just writing about it.

Hundreds of parents laid out gifts under their Christmas Trees the night before. Each parent woke up to an identical scene as when they went to sleep. Cookies and milk were untouched, stockings bulged with undisturbed treats, and gifts rested in their places under the Christmas trees, cold from the lack of children's joy. My wife Nina and I were no exception.

I remember us tiptoeing past our son's bedroom as we carried his gifts from Santa down the hall. Nina was tipsy on eggnog, and I had a bit of a holiday buzz going myself. We giggled and shushed each other as we stumbled through the house. It's one of my best memories, because it's the last time we ever laughed together. Hell, I can't even remember if we've laughed at all since then.

Ronnie was sleeping in his bed as he always was. I know this because my wife and I bickered about her going in there to give him a goodnight kiss. Looking back now, I thank God that she won that battle. It brings me something close to a hint of solace to know that some of his last moments in this house were spent under his mother's love.

We set up his tricycle; placing the largest yellow bow atop the handlebars that we could find. Nina's mother's tradition dictated that we place an orange at the bottom of his stocking; but the rest was filled with little toys and candy. I groaned as she handed me the full plate of cookies.

"Ugh, why do we always make so many again?" I joked.

"Because it's fun! I don't know about you, but when Ronnie and I are making them, a small part of me actually believes they'll be eaten by Father Christmas," she blushed as she placed an amber strand of hair behind her dainty ear.

The thick peanut butter cups atop the cookies were killing me that year. I remember choking on my own saliva; turned into a biting syrup by sugar. We got it done though, leaving exactly one cookie uneaten for Ronnie to sneak in the morning. The milk, however, was all mine.

We awoke to the sounds of sirens and the sun shining through our windows. Nina's bedside clock read 9:18 AM. As much as I tried to fight it, a cold chill enveloped each cell in my body. We knew something was wrong. It's not normal for Ronnie to sleep past 7 o'clock, but especially not on Christmas.

Nina took off running to his room on instinct, fearing that he'd left the house and gotten hit by a car or injured. I held my breath, praying to hear his sleepy little voice. But so far, my wife's calls have gone unanswered.

"Chris! Ronnie's not here," she yelled down the hall.

"What do you mean he's not here? You haven't even checked the living room."

"CHRIS, I'm telling you our baby's not fucking here!" She choked out through sobs. Her footsteps boomed through the house, and I heard the front door slam shut as she left.

My breaths started coming in faster and larger puffs as I tried to process the quickly unfolding situation. The robe I wore the night before was disgusting on my skin. Nothing felt right. It's like at that moment, I already knew that the joy in my life was over. I just couldn't accept it.

Thousands of scenarios invaded my rationality from the corners I'd done so well at keeping them hidden in. Each fear I've ever had as a parent that was always out of reach for someone like me was now all too tangible.

When I opened my front door, I was met with an overwhelming number of sobs and wails. Dozens of people on our street were outside of their homes. Most of them were crying hysterically, some wore blank expressions of shock. Others demanded to search every person's home on the block who didn't have children.

I held my wife as she tumbled to the ground. An officer had told her every child in the county had gone missing Christmas Eve night. My brain fought with itself as to how I should feel. On one hand, hundreds of children kidnapped at the same time would be hard to house and even harder to hide. On the other hand, though, the irrational part of my mind told me that something unnatural had happened altogether, and none of us would ever see our children again.

As the months went on and the seasons changed, most of the parents in town had reached the same heart rendering conclusion, until this morning.

Nina and I are still married, though we sleep in separate bedrooms now. She got on this kick right away about trying for another baby, which I was... am fully against.

First off, I felt that if we had another child, we would be replacing Ronnie. Even worse, we'd be accepting the fact that he was never coming back. We didn't know that. I always held out heartbreaking hope that they'd find him; find all of the missing kids.

Secondly, if something in this town was taking children, I certainly didn't want to give them a new target. Nina's screams woke me from a heavily medicated sleep.

"Chris, it's Ronnie! He's home!"

The covers are thrown in a corner of the room as I spring out of my now cold bed. Each step closer to my son fills my heart with a happiness I feared I no longer possessed. The long lost and dearly missed sound of his voice stops me cold. Whoever is talking to Nina is not our little boy. His voice sounds low and detached; like it's being run through a voice synthesizer.

My stomach heaves when I finally bring myself to finish taking the steps to his bedroom. A mutilated, mangled body lay in the bed that was once meant for our son. Don't get me wrong, he is alive and healthy. He just came back... wrong.

His face is a mingle of features that seem random at best. It was as if Picasso had genetically designed a human being and brought them to life. Licorice whip braids of pink scarring surround his every joint, knuckle and limb. One leg is shorter than the other by six inches. His left arm is thinner and four shades lighter than his right. The left eye placed haphazardly on his face is one of the only qualities that proves to me it's really him. The eye on the right looks like it belongs to someone else entirely.

Once again, the street is thick with police officers, but fire rescue is here this time too. Parents are holding disfigured children as they're laid on stretchers. Each one yelling about how they're fine and don't need treatment. I caught eyes with the little girl who lived across the street from us, and I recognized one of them as my son's.

Whatever happened, it's as if each child was put into a machine, had their DNA all mixed and randomized, then spit back out. The children walk, talk, eat and play like they always have. It's almost impossible to tell who is who anymore.

This Christmas, I'm hearing whispers of a reckoning of sorts. The town leaders and religious figures have labeled these children, some of them their own, as abominations. I've heard there will be a massive event to return the children to the melting pot from which they came.

I'm telling you all this as a warning and for proof for Ronnie down the line to know that his Dad and Mom love him, and never regret a single thing about who he is. We're taking him the hell out of here. By the time they notice a child's missing, we will be long gone. Surely there's somewhere in the World that will greet him with acceptance and love. We're just happy to have him back. Though, I can't help but wonder what surprises Nina and I will wake up to this Christmas morning.

WAITING FOR SANTA

Salt coated the entire inside of my mouth as I took a bite of my enchilada. I'd have choked on my own spit if the salt hadn't evaporated it all. A trail of white lead from the edge of my plate across the counter, leading to an opened, knocked over salt shaker. Fucking Evan! My mind screams at me to yell, to grab him by the arm, spank his ass and lead him off to his bedroom. But... he's only two, and it's Christmas Eve.

The clock read 1:38pm and my heart broke at the realization that my husband wouldn't be home for almost five more hours. I could hear my two older boys distantly arguing in the other room, shortening my patience with every word. It wasn't long before our middle son, Logan, came running up to me, tears streaming down his chubby cheeks. "Mom! Aidan said Santa Claus isn't real. He said that you and Daddy are the ones that eat the cookies and put the presents under our tree."

In the time it had taken him to explain the situation, Evan had disappeared from sight. I was checking the bathroom to make sure he wasn't flushing new rolls of toilet paper again when I heard the sound of glass breaking from my bedroom. I ran across the house, asking Logan to follow me so we could talk along the way. I'd hoped the baby hadn't hurt himself, but I more so hoped that he didn't make a mess of our room.

I found him sitting in the middle of my bed, pointing towards the middle of the floor. He'd taken my makeup mirror and thrown it across the room, it shattered upon impact with the hardwood flooring. Luckily the broom was sitting in the corner of the room closest to me. I grabbed it, instructed Logan to wait in the doorway, and began cleaning up the mess. "Alright sweetie... first of all as much as I hate to say it, your father and I can't afford to fake up a batch of presents for three kids. Think about it for a minute. When we go to the store and you ask for things, what do I say?"

He looked up at me sadly before responding. "You always say not right now, we can't afford it."

As much as I hoped he'd come to this conclusion, it still hurt like a bitch to hear him come out and say it. But... I swallowed my pride and nodded my head convincingly as I emptied the dustpan into the garbage and tied the bag. "Don't you worry," I assured him. "Santa saw and heard that entire conversation. And if your brother doesn't believe well... then, he just won't get as many presents as you, now will he?"

"Do you promise he will come by the house tonight, Momma?" He asked me hopefully.

"Of course he will, sweetheart! Aidan thinks he knows everything, but I promise you he doesn't. I love you. Go get some rest, alright? We all have a big day tomorrow."

My husband arrived home about an hour after all three of the boys went to bed. We ate most of the cookies, and he drank all of the milk. Their presents and stockings were placed lovingly under the tree to be ready for them in the morning. Or in the middle of the night if they decided to be cheeky.

Aidan and Evan bounced into our bedroom before the sun even thought to rise the next morning. As excited as we were for them to open their presents, something felt off as we took our first steps into the living room. The house was freezing cold, and I was shocked to see the front door cracked slightly open.

My husband informed me that Logan wasn't in his room, running up to me with a piece of yellow construction paper in his hand. Our seven-year-old had drawn a picture of himself outside, riding away from our driveway in Santa's sleigh. The words: Be Back Soon, waiting for Santa, were scrawled sloppily in black marker across the top of the page, next to Logan's telltale signature.

The paper fell from my hands as I rushed outside, screaming his name the entire way. All strength fled my knees as I took in the scene of my front yard. A little boy's sock prints could be seen leading up to the middle of the yard, stopping abruptly where fresh tire tracks had ended. The Steamboat Willie Mickey Mouse that he usually had with him at bedtime lay dirty and discarded in the middle of a mud puddle.

Our son had gotten a ride from someone, but unfortunately for all of us... it wasn't Santa.

SPIRALING
DOWN
DISTURBING HORROR STORIES BY
MICHAEL MARKS

"STRIKING, BITING, AND WICKED;
YOU WON'T WANT TO MISS THIS COLLECTION."
PLASTIC
FACES
UNSETTLING STORIES BY
MARTA ABROMAITYTE

"STORIES THAT ARE
GUARANTEED TO
ENTERTAIN"
VACANCY
R.K. KOMBRINCK
THESE LONELY
PLACES

I'VE DONE
THIS
"TRULY SPECIAL"
BEFORE
A BARRAGE OF
NIGHTMARES BY RYAN MAJOR

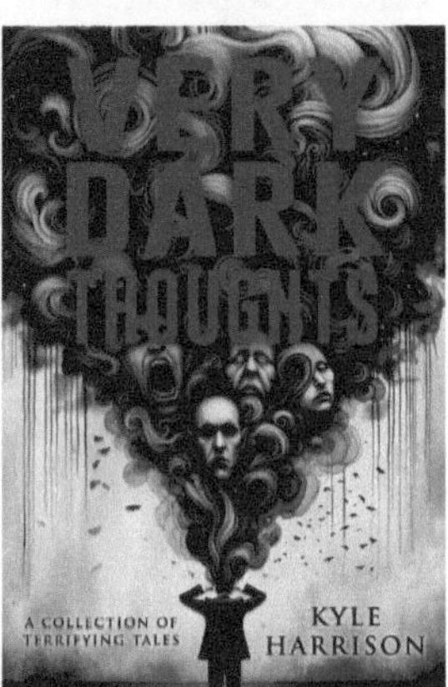

VERY
DARK
THOUGHTS
A COLLECTION OF
TERRIFYING TALES
KYLE
HARRISON

"AN EXCELLENT
COLLECTION
OF HORRORS"
IRON
MAIDENS
TWISTED TALES OF KILLER WOMEN
SARAH JANE HUNTINGTON

STRANGE
TALES
OF THE
MACABRE
TALES BY E. REYES

FACE DOWN
"A GREAT LITTLE
COLLECTION OF THE
BIZARRE [AND]
MACABRE..."
IN THE
GRAVE
SINISTER TALES BY
THOMAS O.

TRIPPING
"T. W. GRIM CAN
TELL ONE HELL OF
A STORY"
OVER
TWILIGHT
DARK TALES BY
T.W. GRIM